Sapphic Confessions

24 Kinky Lesbian Sex Stories

GISELLE RENARDE

Cover design © 2015 Giselle Renarde
First Edition March 2015

ISBN-13: 978-1508881780
ISBN-10: 1508881782

I kissed a girl... and I didn't stop there!

Twenty-four eye-opening lesbian tales so titillating you won't be able to resist reading the next confession. Butches, femmes, chapstick lesbians, bisexual beauties, experienced older women and curious first-timers admit to their naughty deeds in this hot new short story collection.

- **Bad girls get caught being naughty in church.**
- **A bi femme gets spanked by a butch stranger in her pool's sauna room.**
- **An established couple hires a gorgeous girl for a first-time threesome.**
- **A fiery motorcycle dyke makes a scene outside a lesbian nightclub.**
- **An incorrigible house painter converts rich MILFs in their own homes.**
- **Driving lessons get dirty on a dusty country road.**

All this and so much more in Sapphic Confessions: 24 Kinky Lesbian Sex Stories!

Giselle Renarde's erotic fiction has appeared in over 100 anthologies, including prestigious collections like Best Lesbian Erotica, Best Lesbian Romance, Best Women's Erotica, Girl Fever, and the Lambda Award-winning collection Wild Girls, Wild Nights.

TABLE OF CONFESSIONS

-1-
AND KIMI MAKES THREE

There's a bit of truth in the old joke that lesbian sex is just a quiet cup of tea in a room full of cats.

It doesn't start out that way. I can only speak from experience, but when Jody and I first started dating, it was fire. We were so hot for each other back then. I couldn't keep my hands off her ass or my mouth off her tits. She would spend hours between my legs, licking my clit, thrusting her fingers up my snatch. God, it was amazing.

But that was a long time ago. After eight years together, Jody and I had regular sex, but... I don't want to say it was *boring*. Okay maybe it was, just a little.

That sounds mean, I know. I don't intend it that

way. I love Jody more than I've ever loved anyone.

Anyway, one weekend Jody and I checked out the arts and crafts show that's held every summer in our neighbourhood. We didn't need anything, but Jody spotted this vase at a pottery vendor, and she picked it up. Typical lesbian weekend.

It wasn't until we got home that Jody realized the vendor had wrapped her ceramics in one of those free newspapers with all the sex ads in the back: six pages of "Asian Escorts and Massage."

Wow, those photos got my temperature on the rise!

Jody and I fell onto the couch so close our thighs touched. We opened the newspaper and ogled page after page of young women in sexy lingerie.

The girls presented themselves in a variety of pin-up poses. Some smiled coyly or hugged their tits. My favourites were the bold ones, the girls who grabbed their firm little breasts and held them up, on display for everyone to see. Breasts always were my weakness. Some of them leaned forward and pouted their lips, so you didn't know whether to stare at their cleavage or their pretty pink mouths.

And, God, those mouths! Every time I blinked, I saw pretty Asian girls between my legs. I wanted them all.

"Do you think these pictures are real?" Jody asked me.

I couldn't speak. My breath was taken away by the sheer beauty of those girls. What was it about them? Their mock-innocence? Their sexy schoolgirl outfits? The bikini tops that rose so high on their tits the fabric scarcely clung to their nipples? I was getting wet just looking at those slutty photos.

The words didn't help. The ads said things like:

100% Horny Playful Asian GFE!

Excellent Service, No Rush, Guaranteed!

Young, Busty, Cute, Anything Goes!

Fun, Friendly, Tight, Juicy!

"Tight and juicy!" Jody read. The words obviously had the same impact on her that they'd had on me. Her eyes sort of glazed over as she read the ads. And then she pointed to a picture of a sweet-faced girl with naked, pendulous breasts.

Her name, according to the paper, was Kimi. There were little stars on the page to disguise her nipples, and she had an open red gingham shirt hanging off her shoulders. I couldn't get over those tits! They couldn't possibly be real, such big breasts on such a little girl.

"Should we?" Jody asked, pointing to the spot where it said: $40 NUDE ORAL.

I wasn't going to pretend I didn't want it. The girls in these ads could get me off any day of the week. I wouldn't hide my desire.

Jody was nervous, so I made the call. It was a cell number and went straight to voicemail, so I left a message. Not a minute later, someone calling herself a "booking agent" phoned back to set up the date. She had a bit of an accent, and I wondered if it was Kimi herself on the phone.

God, those tits—they were all I could think about.

I'd never done this before. I wondered if the girl on the phone would think it was weird that two women were requesting a hooker. Did other lesbians pay for sex? Nobody talked about it, so I assumed it didn't happen.

We set the date for later that evening. I don't think Jody or I could have waited any longer. We would have changed our minds if we'd had to.

We were a bundle of nerves as we waited for Kimi to arrive. I tried catching up on some emails, but I couldn't concentrate. I don't know what Jody was up to. We didn't talk about what might happen. We didn't discuss it at all.

There was a knock at the door, and my spine went arrow-straight. I was sure, absolutely one hundred percent sure, that I was going to have a heart attack.

But I didn't.

I started thinking, "I can't do this, I can't do this..." but even as I thought it, I made my way to the door.

Jody was already there, holding the handle. Just holding it. Just standing there.

I put my hand on hers, and we opened it together.

The girl standing on the other side was pretty as a picture—but *was* she the girl in the picture? Hard to say. Without actually holding the newspaper beside her, I couldn't tell. Maybe once her soft yellow cardigan came off, I'd recognize the tits.

Yes, that's right—our hooker wore a cardigan.

It was cute, actually, with a felt flower pinned to the chest. Her whole outfit reminded me of a 1950's sock-hopper, but with a modern flair. Asian girls had a knack for looking good in quirky outfits. That's something I never could pull off.

When we asked if she was Kimi, the girl nodded demurely. We welcomed her in and she entered, holding her purse and her jacket in front of her. I wondered if she dressed this way for everyone, or if this was something special for the crabby old lesbians. It did make me happy that she wasn't wearing some slutty spandex thing.

"Nude oral?" the girl asked. She held out her hand, and I realized she wanted payment upfront. Then she asked, "One or two?"

I wasn't exactly sure what she meant, but Jody said, "Oh, on both of us. One and then the other."

Kimi smiled as I placed the cash in her hand—ratty, wrinkled twenty-dollar bills with the queen smiling up at us. For the first time ever, I wondered why the Queen of *England* was on Canadian money, and then I chastised myself for thinking about something so irrelevant. There was a prostitute in my living room! I should be... well, I didn't know what I should be doing. Then I started feeling nervous.

I looked to Jody, who smiled at me the way the queen was smiling on the twenty.

My stomach tied itself in knots.

Kimi asked if we were a couple, and Jody responded that we were, but even her voice was trembling now. The girl smiled, and then asked how long we'd been together. It surprised me that she seemed curious about us. I guess I figured we were just money to her, just bodies, but she appeared interested in Jody and I as people, and that really put me at ease.

Her accent was thicker than the girl on the phone, but I could see the enthusiasm in her eyes. She talked about the weather, and about the arts and crafts show—she'd been there as well. Strange to think the girl who was now our hooker had been walking around with the crowds, just one more person.

I guess I'd never thought of prostitutes as real people.

When Kimi asked where we'd like to do it and who wanted to go first, I got nervous again. I felt a little weird about taking my clothes off in front of her. Jody must have felt the same way, because she asked Kimi to strip for us.

In a flash, Kimi's expression went from innocent to saucy. When she grinned, her lip turned up more on one side than the other. That subtle tease made my pussy pound.

Our pretty hooker unbuttoned her cardigan. The tease continued, rendering my legs so wobbly I had to sit down.

Without a bit of shyness, Kimi shrugged off her sweater. That's when I got my first look at her gorgeous tits. The firm cups of her dainty white bra hugged them sweetly. There was just enough lace around her cleavage to shift her lingerie out of the boring zone—not that any garment could truly be boring on a body like hers!

Kimi stepped out of her skirt, giving us a good view of her long, smooth legs. She didn't take off her square heels, and I was glad about that. She reminded me of the naughty librarian who takes the bun out of her hair and becomes a sex goddess.

Bending forward, Kimi grabbed her tits and pressed them together. I couldn't take my eyes off that glorious line of cleavage as she juggled and jiggled her big breasts. God, I wanted to touch myself. I wanted to touch her, too!

"You like my big tits?" Kimi asked as she hypnotized us with the marvellous pair. "You want to touch my big fucking titties?"

"Yeah, yeah." I was panting like a dog as I grabbed her breasts from behind. She sighed, and that sound made me want to come. I missed that enthusiasm for touch, that sensitivity.

She let me strip off her panties, then undo her bra, and when her big boobs tumbled from the cups, I was there to catch them.

I told her to lick Jody's clit. I wanted to hear my woman come while this gorgeous slut ate her cunt.

Jody raced out of her clothes as Kimi sank to the

floor in front of the couch. I went with her, riding her back all the way, hugging her small body as I fondled her amazingly supple, soft tits. Her nipples were hard little pebbles between my fingers, and they were all I could think about until I heard Jody gasp.

Draped over Kimi's naked back, I looked up to see her black hair cascading over one shoulder, her face buried between my partner's thighs. I'd gone down on Jody countless times, but for some reason this was a thousand times more exciting. I watched her lips part. Her mouth opened wide. The sloppy sound of our hooker's wet tongue on my girlfriend's pussy ramped up my arousal so high I released one of Kimi's tits and traced my hand down her back... down her ass crack...

I wasn't sure if I was allowed to do this. Kimi seemed to trust us as much as we were trusting her, so I took a chance and found her with my fingers. The newspaper ad was right—she was incredibly tight, and so wet her juice was dripping down between her legs.

Jody's eyes fluttered closed as Kimi lapped her clit. Our living room filled with body sounds—the wet squelching of my fingers plunging in and out of Kimi's cunt, the sweet lapping of Kimi's tongue on my woman's clit, and our whimpering, moaning, sighing, grunting. We were all so turned on. Three women, just a big ball of juicy female arousal!

I was so jealous of those two, because they'd been

smart enough to take off their clothes early on. Me, I was still fully dressed and wishing my clothing would just melt off my skin. It felt so damn good to have half my hand shoved up Kimi's snatch while she went at Jody's cunt with her mouth.

Jody was kicking and screaming now, loving every moment of our Kimi's tongue teasing her clit. I wanted to watch. I wanted to see Kimi's face buried between my lover's thighs, licking and flicking, sucking that sweet bud like a little cock.

The cravings rose up in me, but I couldn't decide. Did I want to lick or be licked? Suck or be sucked? But then I remembered what I'd paid for, and I figured I might as well get my money's worth.

Tearing out of my clothes, I threw myself beside Jody on the couch. Kimi moved from Jody's pussy to mine, like a baby shifting from one breast to the other. Everything felt otherworldly, like a dream. Real life was never this good, never this easy. I had a gorgeous young woman between my legs, naked, with the biggest damn tits I'd ever seen up close and personal, and what did it take to get her there? Nothing, really. Just a little phone call, just a little cash. It was too good to be true.

Sliding two long fingers into my pussy, Kimi rubbed my g-spot enough to warm my whole pelvis. I couldn't believe how close I was to orgasm already. All the watching and waiting had turned me on like crazy, and I knew the moment her tongue met my clit I was going to blow.

I watched her pretty face as she drew in close. She kissed my clit, so gentle, so sweet, like a butterfly landing briefly on my skin and then taking right off again. She looked up at me and smiled, but I growled back at her. I wasn't angry or anything, I was just so aroused I couldn't control myself. At all! Grabbing her by the hair, I shoved my slick pussy against her face, which was already soaked with Jody's juice. I rubbed off on her mouth while she squirmed and squealed.

I know I said things to her while my body worked itself into a frenzy of orgasm. "Yeah, you like that, huh? You love the taste of my hot fucking cunt, don't you?" Stuff like that. Stuff I never said to Jody.

Kimi just kept nodding, gulping, gasping, saying, "Uh-huh! Uh-huh!"

The look in her eyes put me over the top. She was scared or something. Cautious, maybe, like she was trying to gauge if I was a danger to her.

I wasn't, of course. I wasn't a danger to anyone, but I scoured my pussy against Kimi's beautiful face until I'd come in crashing waves, over and over, and I couldn't take any more pleasure. Then she backed away, fixing her hair and smiling guardedly between Jody and me.

We thanked her and she thanked us, kneeling on the floor like some kind of sexual servant. After she'd gone, my woman and I sat naked on the couch holding hands for literally hours. In all that time, I kept looking down and expecting to see Kimi there like a toy poodle, wanting to serve us, wanting to bring us happiness and contentment. I hope she knows what she did for Jody and me, because that girl revived us. She really did.

Thank you Kimi, wherever you are.

-2-
ARE YOU MY MOMMY?

I never realized I wanted to be spanked until the day I called my girlfriend "Mom."

Actually, I'd called Louisa "Mom" many times before, but always in my trademark self-reflexive mock-teenager tone. For instance, she might ask me to please eat something healthy for dinner and I might say, "Yes, *Mom*," or she might comment on what a mess my apartment was and I might say, "I'll clean it tomorrow, *Mom*." It was conscious and innocuous and always, always a joke.

This "Mom" was different.

In truth, I can't recall what I was so worked up about at the time. Something career-related, most likely. I remember Louisa sitting on the edge of my bed, fully dressed. I was nearly naked and standing between her thighs. My arms rested on her shoulders, my body nestled into the warm comfort of her cleavage as I whined about whatever the trouble was. She ran her hands through my hair in consolation and suddenly I said, "I don't know what to do about it, Mom."

I didn't hear it until after I'd said it, and by that time, of course, I couldn't take it back. My spine straightened, vertebra by vertebra, until I was standing straight as an arrow.

"Did you hear that?" I asked. "I just called you Mom."

Louisa didn't react at all the way I expected. She just laughed and said, "Freud would have a field day."

"You're not...?" *Not what?* Angry? Upset? Afraid? I didn't even know what I was asking. "I mean, that's weird. Right? Calling my girlfriend Mom?"

"Do you love me?"

"Yes."

She held my hands, swinging them out to the sides. "And you love your mother?"

"Of course I do."

"And your mother and I are basically the same age?"

I hesitated, which was stupid because it was a rhetorical question. Louisa knew very well she was nearly as old as my mother. Hell, she had more in common with my mom than she had with me. Sometimes I thought if we ever broke up… well, that was silly. Louisa would be mine forever.

"You're not mad?" I asked, feeling beyond juvenile. That was such a childish question, but I couldn't think of a better one in the moment.

She ran her hands over the curve of my ass, squeezing. "Why would I be mad?"

Luckily, Louisa had always been one of those super-mature partners who didn't mind listening to stories about other lovers. So I said, "My ex would have freaked out."

Her blue eyes sparkled like aquamarines, and the knowing smile on her lips told me she understood. Even so, she cocked her head and asked, "Why?"

"Because of the age difference." I ran my fingers across Louisa's lips until she nipped at me and I pulled away, laughing. "She was a year older than you, and she always worried people would think I was her daughter."

I took a chance then, leaning in to kiss my girl. She didn't bite me this time. She returned my kiss, slow and sensual, her tongue mingling with mine like two sizzling serpents. That day I had on my black velvet camisole, the one with the black lace across the top, and Louisa took hold of the straps, pulling them down my arms until the stretchy fabric rested around my hips.

"Why did she care?" Louisa asked as I crawled into her lap, straddling her broad thighs.

"Hmm?"

"Your ex." She cupped my naked breasts. The warmth of her palms on my not-yet-hard nipples made me moan. "Why did she care so much what other people thought?"

"Oh, it wasn't just other people." Normally I wouldn't have been keen on discussing old relationships in bed with my new girlfriend, but there was something about Louisa that just opened me up. I wanted to reveal myself, in all my imperfect glory. "It's like she was afraid of what we thought of ourselves, or afraid of all the hidden stuff inside our heads. If you think I'm Jungian, she was, like, ultra-Jungian with a hint of Freudian guilt in there somewhere."

Louisa looked me in the eye while her hands pulsed against my breasts, and I knew she had no idea what I was talking about.

I tried again. "There were things she wouldn't do because they played too much into the age dynamic. Anything that came close to age play was totally out of bounds. If I'd called her Mommy in the bedroom she would have been upset. If I'd slipped like I did just now and called her Mom by accident? Jesus, I think her head would have exploded. She would have run a mile."

"See, I don't get that." Louisa let out a little growl as she pinched my nipples, then rolled them between her fingers and thumbs until I squealed. "Everybody brings a parent/child dynamic to romantic relationships. Even if we were the same age, that dynamic would be there to a certain extent. It's just accentuated with us because I'm older and you're younger."

"I know," I said, hissing gently. She still hadn't let go of my tits. "I agree with you, but my ex was ridiculously afraid I wanted her to be my mother, or that I saw her that way, or... well, whatever."

"And did you?" Louisa asked idly, like the question was insignificant.

Something inside me froze while my body jerked forward. Before I knew what I was doing, I'd shoved my tits in Louisa's face, rubbing my pebbled little nipples against her lips. God, that felt good, the way they sort of stuck to her tacky lipstick, picking up traces of the stuff. Soon enough my tits had gone from subtle pink to shimmering reddish-brown.

"Aren't you going to suck my tits?" I took her head in my hands, tempting her with one breast and then the other.

She smiled that impish smile I knew so well. "Is that what you want?"

"Yes."

I didn't think she'd do it, at least not right away. I thought she'd tease me a little longer, running her lips side to side across my tits, maybe licking them with that hot velvet tongue. But I was wrong. Louisa wrapped her mouth around my breast, overshooting my nipple and sucking half my little boob into her big bad mouth.

"Oh baby!" When she bit my pursed nipple, I wrapped my hands around her head and moaned. "God, you're good at this."

She switched sides, glancing up at me before taking my other tit in her mouth. "So, what would your ex have done if you'd asked for a spanking?"

I laughed, because never in a million years would she have gone for that. "She probably would have explained to me, very calmly, that spanking would feel too much like a mother disciplining her daughter and she wasn't interested in exploring that realm of our relationship."

"What about you?" Louisa's mouth hovered over my nipple, and her warm breath made my pussy ache. "Were you interested in exploring that realm of your relationship?"

"Hmm?" I found it hard to focus with her mouth so close to my breast. "With her? Not really. We had good sex, so I was happy."

I nudged my tit at Louisa's lips, but she turned to look at me. "What about with us? How would you like it if I spanked you?"

My pussy clamped down on nothing and my heart beat fast. "You would do that?"

Louisa shrugged, suddenly indifferent, though I knew it was an act. "If that's what you wanted, sure."

"I want you to suck my tits," I said, forcing my breast against her mouth until she opened up at last.

When she wrapped those perfect lips around my nipple, my pussy begged for attention. "Oh God, baby, can you fingerfuck me too?"

"You sure do ask for a lot," she mumbled without drawing completely away from my breast.

"That's because you're so good at everything."

My blatant flattery worked, and Louisa snuck one hand between my thighs. She felt around, tracing her soft fingers up and down my slit before entering me from behind. I arched forward, shoving my breast into her mouth as she fucked me. One finger at first, then two. Three of her large fingers were really all I could bear in my tight little cunt, and when she pumped them inside me I bucked back against them, wanting more, always more.

Even though she'd just asked me if I wanted a spanking, I admit I wasn't ready when her heavy hand fell against my ass.

I gasped, straightening up, looking her plain in the eye. She was smiling, of course.

"You didn't like that?" she asked.

"I... did." I couldn't move. Thank goodness Louisa had a grip on my waist to keep me from toppling over. "That was my first spanking, you know."

"I know." She spanked me again. "And that was your second."

At first I wasn't clear on which hand she'd used, but when I felt my pussy juice slathered across my ass I realized her fingers were no longer inside me.

That's when I knew she must have spanked me with the hand she'd used to fingerfuck me.

I let myself go and tumbled against Louisa, hooking my chin over her shoulder. She was so steady, so reliable. When Louisa was around, I knew I was safe.

Her hand struck my ass again, and this third spanking was the first I remember actually feeling. The first two were novelty, pure fun, but this one slammed my skin unforgivingly, making me wince.

"Oh God, Louisa." I kissed her neck, sucking skin that tasted faintly of pressed powder and salt. "That was amazing."

"What, this?" She spanked me again, same spot, and a dull burn began. When I closed my eyes, I could see her red handprint on my ass. She'd left her mark.

And again, another clout.

"You like this?" she asked.

"God, yes." I bit her shoulder as she brought her hot palm down on my ass once again, keeping it there when the blow was struck. I couldn't believe how my skin blazed, how hard she was smacking me. "That feels so good."

"You like getting spanked?" She rubbed both her palms around both my cheeks, teasing me before slapping my ass with two hands. "You like getting spanked by Mommy?"

It sounded weird. It sounded so weird I didn't know how to respond.

"No?" she asked.

"I…" What could I say? I wanted her to keep going. "I like it. A lot."

"Oh you do?" She smacked my ass again, the right cheek, then the left, right, left, alternating until it burned so badly I reached behind to shield myself from the blows.

"If you like it, why are you blocking your ass?"

"It hurts," I said, thinking that would be enough to stop her.

No chance. Louisa pulled my hands away and spanked my ass again. "I thought you liked getting spanked by Mommy."

"By you!" I cried, trying to cover my ass. "Not by Mommy, by you!"

"By me?" she asked, sounding all sweet and innocent as she ripped my hands away from my bum. "You want to be spanked by *me*?"

She didn't wait for an answer. Louisa walloped my blazing ass. One spanking, two, three, four. I lost count because my head wouldn't stop buzzing. "It hurts! Baby, it hurts! It hurts so bad…"

"And you like it?"

Tears pricked my eyes. I felt hot all over. "Yes!"

"And you want more?"

I struggled and writhed against her, but I couldn't escape her grip. "I want more!"

Louisa spanked me and I arched against her frame as if she would protect me from herself. "You like it, don't you?"

"It hurts!" I hollered, releasing the tears that had welled in my eyes. They streamed down my cheeks as I screamed with the pain of every new blow.

I squirmed like a rabbit trying to escape a child's grip, but it was no use. Louisa held me firmly in place as she whacked my tender ass. My skin was so red and hot and hurting it almost felt like it wasn't part of my body anymore.

"If you've had enough, just say 'enough' and I'll stop." Louisa struck me yet again, and I wanted to say it but I couldn't. It was the strangest feeling, wanting more and wanting it to end.

Every spanking was torture now. I was crying, actually crying, and still I couldn't ask her to stop.

Suddenly we were on the move, and I clung to Louisa's shoulders because I thought I was falling. No, not falling...sliding? Louisa pulled me up on the bed and shifted until she was lying on her back and I was snuggled into her front.

The spankings seemed to have stopped, but still I felt on edge. They'd begun so abruptly and continued so forcefully that I couldn't be sure those pretty palms of hers had finished their work.

After a few long breaths, Louisa arched to my ear and whispered, "I think you've had enough."

A smile of relief bled across my lips as my body melted into hers. "Thank God! That hurt like a bitch, but I couldn't ask you to stop."

"You couldn't ask your mommy to stop or you couldn't ask your girlfriend to stop?"

I smirked against her shoulder, closing my eyes. My cheeks were still wet with tears, and my ass burned like the fires of hell. I was naked and sweating and aroused and satisfied all at once.

"You're not going to answer that question, are you?" Louisa teased.

She knew me too well. "Of course not."

-3-
ARTISTS' WIVES

I'd always had a thing for artists.

What was it about them? Not their looks—that's for sure. Didn't matter what a guy looked like, whether he was embarrassingly young or decrepitly old, big or small in any direction. If he was an artist, I was into him. From afar. I never had the confidence to actually approach a guy. I figured I wasn't an artist's type.

So my friend Luxanne hooked me up with some work as a life model. She'd been doing it for years and told me what to expect. *Nothing.*

"You hear all this bullshit about painters seducing naked girls on velvet sofas," she said. "Pure romanticism. Never happens."

23

And if it never happened to her, there was no way in hell it would happen for me. Luxanne was slim and blonde, undeniably desirable. I was pretty much the opposite of that.

I gave it a shot nonetheless, with my hopes sky-high. A private session, too—none of that posing for a class of students stuff. I stripped bare, I laid my naked self out, but Master Reinhardt didn't take the bait. He was all business, all brushes and oils. I could see it in his eyes. No lust there. And I felt pretty crappy about that, even though he was rather old and not what most women would call handsome. None of that mattered. He was an artist, and that made me all butterfly-bellied the whole time I was sitting for him. Even though he was looking at me completely naked, I felt like he wasn't really seeing me at all. Maybe he was gay. I secretly hoped he was, just so this wouldn't be a case of yet another man gazing right past me. Why was I invisible?

The great master set down his brush and looked me in the eye. Would he make a move now? My heart raced. *See me! Love me! Want me!*

No such luck.

"I have business to attend to." His voice was dark and rough, like gravel. It made me tingle all over, especially below my belly. "My wife Ethel will bring your luncheon. Please pardon my absence. I shall return post haste."

"Okay, sure." He'd already left the room by the

time I said, "No problem."

I wasn't sure where to go, or if this wife of his was bringing lunch to me. Hell, I couldn't even remember where I'd put my clothes! I definitely wanted to get dressed before some old lady came in the room and spotted me in my birthday suit.

Too late.

A wheeled cart pushed the studio door open, squealing as it entered the room. Behind it stood a young Asian woman with long black hair tucked behind her ears. She had on a tight black T-shirt and frayed jogging pants covered in paint.

"Hey." She sounded uninspired, like she'd rather be any place but here. "Lunch."

There was a spring salad on the cart, with cherry tomatoes and little bocconcini balls alongside grilled chicken. It looked amazing. So did she. I didn't want to admit my attraction, even to myself, but I couldn't deny that tingle between my legs.

Artists…they did it for me every time.

Still, I felt jumpy and weird with this stranger seeing me naked.

"Sorry." Should I cover my boobs and my bush? No, she'd think I was an idiot. "Master Reinhardt said his wife was bringing me lunch."

She raised an eyebrow, seeming unamused in the extreme. "Okay."

"You're obviously an artist too." I didn't know why I was talking. I felt so stupid. "Do a lot of artists work out of the house?"

"A few." She shrugged. "Students use the extra studio space in exchange for household chores, a little cooking and cleaning. It's a pretty good deal."

Ahh, so this girl was an art student! My pussy pulsed as I looked at the globs of paint coating her clothes. What was it about artists? God, there was even paint on her bare arms. She was irresistible!

Stretching out on the sofa, I said, "I'm Tara."

"Okay."

She turned, and I was sure she would leave, but she didn't. She locked the door! I couldn't believe it. My belly did flip-flops as she inched between the master's canvas and the lunch cart, coming toward me.

"You're naked," she said.

I could hardly breathe. The look in her eyes, that dark lusty look, made me feel jittery and scared. I didn't know why.

"That's quite a bush." She was staring at my pussy.

I was so embarrassed I just wanted to die! "I'm sorry."

She laughed and shook her head. "No, I like it. I'm sick of shaved pussies. You don't see a nice thick pelt very often these days. Girls are so ashamed of their hair."

Something inside me clicked from no to yes, and I lifted my arms to show her I didn't shave there either.

"Wow." She nodded, and the look in her eyes

was so ruthless I really didn't know what would happen next. My guess was she was about to jump on me, but she didn't. She just looked. *Stared*.

I let my arms fall at my sides. The words came out of nowhere: "Do you want me?"

Her eyebrow went up. "Do you want me to want you?"

"Yes." I'd never been so forward in all my life. "I want you to lick me."

"Where?" She was playing with me, teasing, taunting.

I was too turned on to play games. With two fingers, I spread my pussy lips to show her the glistening pink inside. I'd been wet all morning. "Here."

She smiled, a half-smile, like half of her was deliriously happy and the other half was aching with desire. That's how I felt, too. I would have begged if she weren't so willing.

When I opened my legs, setting one bare foot up on the sofa, she fell to her knees like my pussy was a force she just couldn't resist. I wanted to feel humiliated that this beautiful student had commented on my pubic hair, obviously comparing me mentally with all the other women she'd been with, but instead I felt strangely proud.

She stared straight into my pussy as I held my lips open for her. My heart clamped as I awaited her reaction. I felt hot and cold in pulses. Waves of heat and ice soared through my body.

"Please." I couldn't wait any longer. "Lick me."

I watched her full lips open and her pink tongue emerge, soft as velvet. Her black hair shone like oil streams against her washed-out cotton T-shirt. It felt like millennia as her mouth approached my pussy, like she was moving in slow motion. Maybe she was.

And then her tongue met my clit, and I felt it like a sizzling streak through my core. Throwing my head back, I whimpered, trying not to buck up and smack my wet pussy against her nose. It was hard to keep still. My body wanted to move, wanted to rock and writhe against her face. She had so much to give me—I could see it in her eyes.

When she dove at my pussy, I gasped, struggling to hold my lips open for her. Were my knuckles pummelling her nose? Did my pussy taste good? Was it sweet or was it musky, or could she taste only my juice? So much it was dripping down my ass crack, probably soaking Master Reinhardt's sofa. I'd have a lot of explaining to do when he came back.

But right now all I cared about was this sensation, her tongue lapping my clit in quick strokes. I'd never been licked by another woman. The sensation defied belief. She wasn't slow and steady, not at all. She attacked my cunt like she was running out of time, like she needed me to come right now.

I felt all the energy drain from my shoulders. My hands went numb. So did my toes. It all gravitated to my pussy.

My clit felt full and huge, big as a cock, and when she sucked it into her hot mouth I felt like she was giving me a blowjob. I'd never in my life felt so wildly aroused. She gave me everything. Her mouth was my pleasure.

"Oh God!" I couldn't keep quiet. It felt too good. "Yes, please! Suck my clit, suck it harder!"

She did! My God, I wouldn't have believed it was possible, but she somehow managed to suck my clit and my pussy lips into her mouth and devour them en masse.

I couldn't keep quiet and I couldn't keep still. I writhed against her face, still holding my outer lips open for her, trying desperately not to scratch her cheeks with my long fingernails.

"Fuck yeah!" I didn't usually swear like that, not even in bed, but the naughty words came streaming out beyond my control. "Fuck yeah, suck it, baby! Suck my fucking clit. That feels so fucking good you fucking slut!"

I'd never called anyone a slut in my life. I don't know where that came from, but it worked! She growled and shook her head side to side, putting a delicious strain on my clit. I was nothing but a big throbbing pussy being devoured by a beautiful stranger, and that was fine by me.

The edge was so close I could taste it. My climax was an ache pounding at the base of my pelvis, almost in my ass. It swelled each time she sucked and each time I swore, but I knew what would put me over the precipice. I'd been there before.

With my free hand, I pinched the closest nipple and lost all sense of time and place. My feet started kicking above the head between my legs. I knew I was hollering like a fiend, but all I could hear was the rush of my heartbeat, like an ocean in my ears.

My legs began to ache, and I wrapped them around the girl's black cotton back, forcing my pussy flush to her wet face. I couldn't stop myself. I thrust against her mouth, her chin, her cheeks, tracing my pussy juice all across her face until she was dripping with the stuff.

All at once, the pleasure was too much.

I tried to back away, but she kept eating me, kept sucking until I cried out, "Stop! Stop! Oh fuck, you have to stop!"

That's when I heard knocking on the studio door.

For a moment, everything buzzed. The world became too real.

Then I heard Master Reinhardt's voice. "Ethel? Ethel, would you let me inside?"

The girl between my legs glanced at the door, looking rather more nonchalant than I felt.

"Just a sec." Drawing away from my pussy, Ethel murmured, "I wish he'd stay out longer. I never get a turn."

I hadn't moved when she opened the door—I think I was in shock. My legs were still splayed, my pussy dripping juice all down the sofa. I was going to get fired for sure.

But Master Reinhardt simply looked from the food tray by the canvas to me on the sofa. As his wife slipped out the door, he picked up his brush and asked, "You didn't like your salad?"

"It...I...I don't know."

I'd always had a thing for artists.

Now I have a thing for artists' wives.

-4-

BUTCH GIRLS DON'T CRY

There are days when you just have to get out of the house. Or out of the apartment, in my case. I don't know what made *that* day one of *those* days. Call it cabin fever, or sexual frustration, or simply fate. That day, I just had to get out. One problem: the wind was howling, and Channel Three predicted the storm would turn ugly. If I had to get out of the apartment without leaving the building, my only option was the penthouse pool.

I've never been much of a swimmer, but I knew the exercise would do me good. Too much built-up energy in my system. Kicking my legs and flailing my arms would take care of it, I hoped. Plus, I'd bought a lovely little bikini at the end of the summer and I had yet to premiere it. My building was full of hot young guys and gorgeous geek girls—no time like the present to strut my stuff in front of them! Hell, maybe I'd get lucky and some mysterious stranger would take me home like a lost puppy.

When I stepped out of the changing room, the pool area was deserted but for one other person. If I'd seen her from behind, I would have thought for sure she was a man. From the front, it was only the big braless tits under a grey cotton tank top that gave her away. Her face and her middle were pudgy, but her tattooed arms surged with such strength my knees nearly gave out just looking at her. She had short hair, a dusty and indistinct colour, and unshaven legs under big cargo shorts. Her face wore a focused expression as she worked out at the weight machine in the corner. The "gym" in our building got moved into the pool area when the residents' board decided to put saunas in both change rooms. I still hadn't seen the inside of those steamy wooden caverns, just like I'd never seen this butch babe around the building before. The idea of both together made me hot.

As I unwrapped my towel from my nearly naked body, I felt a wicked smile bleed across my lips. Thank God I'd left the apartment today. Thank God I'd worn this bikini. You never know what you're going to find up here at the penthouse level. Could be boys and their toys or girls with their curls…or it could be this butch powerhouse at the weight machine. I knew I was staring, but I didn't care. I'd come up here to see and be seen, and I wouldn't be content until I'd achieved both goals.

From the far end of the pool, I watched the vigorous stranger's iron-pumping pace slow to a crawl. Those hulking arms twitched as she set down her weights. Her gaze fixed on my flesh like laser beams intent on burning off the white halter straps of my bikini top. If only her eyes could cut them loose! I wanted to expose my tits to her then and there, and watch her face harden with desire. There was an intensity to her that I could feel even across the expanse of chlorinated water.

Tossing my towel on a deck chair, I waded into the pool, flicking my long hair over my shoulders. I knew she was watching as my chilled nipples grew hard under my bikini top, but I didn't return her gaze. I didn't want to give her the satisfaction—not just yet. Everybody knows there's an art to this game of seduction.

I plunged my head beneath the cool water and tried to swim gracefully. It had been a while, but I wanted to showcase my lean figure with minimal splashing or thrashing of limbs. I did a damn fine job, I think.

When I'd finished a couple laps I glanced casually toward the weight machine in the corner, ready to tease that hot daddy some more...but she was gone. The weight machine had fallen to disuse. The whole pool area was empty. I couldn't believe my stinging eyes.

Well, she couldn't have gone far. I hopped from the pool, grabbed my towel, and stomped on wet feet to the changing room. Empty. No signs of life or neighbours—granted, most of the people in my building worked during the day—but more importantly, no sign of the striking stranger from the weight machine. I couldn't help feeling insulted. What, I wasn't hot enough for her? Of course I was! How could she resist? No, how *dare* she resist?

I tore out of my bathing suit and tossed it in the direction of my bag before slipping under a hot shower. Wringing out my wet hair, I wrapped the wet towel around my naked middle and figured I might as well cool my jets in the hot sauna.

It wasn't until I'd swung open the heavy wooden door that I realized there was somebody inside. And who do you think that somebody was? Yes indeed, it was the big bad butch who'd caught my eye by the pool and then rejected me. She was fully dressed, but her head hung low. Deep moaning sounds fell from her full lips. Between her feet in black flip-flops, tears sizzled against the hot wooden floor slats. My big strong butch was crying! Not whining like a girl, not whimpering like a puppy, but blubbering like a man. Like her father or her dog just died, as Leonard Cohen put it.

This mysterious stranger had suffered a loss for sure, but I was pretty sure it had nothing to do with a father or a dog. It was a loss in love, that much I could tell. I could feel it in my heart—my heart, which expanded to house her hurt with every breath. I knew just the type of dark-haired beauty who'd trampled her spirit with stiletto boots: deep red lips, bright red nails, short bangs and a vintage dress. A vixen. A tart.

Oh, how many times had that beauty been me?

Tears streamed down her plump cheeks, barely distinguishable from the sweat gleaming on her skin. She didn't acknowledge me, except by sitting up a little straighter. Still, her chin swung down close to her chest. As she shook her head left and right, tears soaked the front of her sweat-dampened tank top. She mumbled indistinguishable words, but I got the sense she wasn't talking to me or even to herself. My guess? She was pleading with the woman now absent from her life, the pretty girl who'd hurt her so damn badly.

Everybody knows a break-up cry. You know it when you see it. Because we've all been there, everybody above the age of sixteen or so. We've all been hit by that bolt from the blue, or seen the end slowly creeping up on us like a creature of the night. And it hurts. God, it hurts like nothing else in the world and it leaves us weak as kittens. Time may heal the wound of this individual experience, but the next time a relationship comes to an end, we're torn open just as wide. There's no learning curve for emotion. We are subjected to it and rendered submissive in its hands.

I'm no mother, but I know what it is to care for another human being. My maternal instinct is strong enough to embrace anyone in need, and open enough to realize the desire that care can generate. Open enough not to turn that desire away. Open enough to welcome it. So I walked across the sauna room. All it took was three small steps.

When I stood before her, she covered her face with both hands. She leaned so far forward her head nearly met my middle. She set her elbows against her knees, and her strong shoulders shook as she sobbed. Her whole body seemed to rattle, which gave her a skeletal appearance despite her bulk.

I couldn't resist any longer. I had to touch her.

Easing forward, I set my hands gently against her heaving shoulders. Her bare skin was slick with sweat, and her muscles twinged under my touch. As I traced my palms down her big biceps and then up her straining neck, she leaned her head into my soft body. The moment I felt her face against my belly, a gush of warmth flooded my heart. Running my fingernails through the short hair at the back of her head, I whispered all the words of comfort my mother would have said to me.

"*Shh shh shh*, now. This too shall pass, and all shall be well with the world."

In time, her sobbing subsided. When I felt in my heart she trusted me, I pried her hands from her face and wiped the tears from her cheek with my thumb. I even ran my hand underneath my towel and wiped her nose, because that's what a good mommy would do. And that's when she finally looked up at me.

Her glistening hazel eyes were bloodshot from crying. The droplets clinging to her lower lashes sparkled, even in the sauna room's low light. Yes, her whole face was tearstained and red, but there was a masculine beauty to the sadness painted across her skin. She allowed me to see the wounded child behind the rough exterior, and nothing could have touched me more.

Unwrapping my towel, I held it end to end like a set of angel wings as I revealed my nakedness to her. Her gaze descended my body, drizzling down my chest like hot fudge before settling on my bare tits. My towel slipped from my fingers and fell to the hot wooden floor. Taking her head in my hands, I offered myself to her in thought and in action.

As I stepped close, she tipped her head upward. She set her face against my bare breast and my whole body burned to heal her pain. When she rubbed her wet cheek against my naked flesh, I traced my fingers down her neck.

Like a babe at her mother's breast, she sought my nipple with her lips. Though her eyes were now closed, she found it with no trouble. Taking my tit inside her hot mouth, she suckled. She sucked rhythmically, as though my body were singing her a lullaby, and I felt my pussy grow slick as I soothed her.

Juice soaked my thighs, and she knew it as soon

as I did. Wrapping one powerful arm around my waist, she pulled me into her broad lap. Her damp cargo shorts felt rough against my smooth ass, but her sudden movement no less enthralled me. She'd been such a predictable beast until now.

Switching sides to suck my other breast, she cast her hand between my legs. She plunged her fingers down the length of my pussy lips and hissed when she felt the wetness she'd inspired. For short hair, hers was so soft I couldn't keep my fingers out of it. I stroked the nape of her neck while she stroked my clit, and I honestly don't know who derived more enjoyment from the interplay of fingers and flesh.

Her touch made my stomach flutter. Every time she stroked my clit, my pelvis bucked up at her hand. She pushed me back down until my ass sat firm on her thigh. With every rub, my pussy leaped forward a little higher and she pushed it back down a little harder, until my buck became a thrust and her stroke became a slap. The blood in my veins seemed to sizzle as her smacks landed against my engorged clit. My abdomen quaked every time she struck me with those firm, fat fingers.

The heat of the sauna was catching up with me, and my chest glistened with sweat. I prayed to the sauna gods this wounded stranger would never stop sucking my tits. The movements of her mouth corresponded perfectly to the actions of her hands and she looked damn good doing it. She turned her head side to side, rolling it in cyclical motions as she drew my nipple into a bud between her lips. When she nibbled at my flesh, electricity coursed through my veins and my pussy surged toward the ceiling. She smacked it back down, and it sprang right up again.

She growled as she chewed on my tits and whacked my wet pussy with her hand. The sound was so fierce it should have scared me. Maybe it did scare me just a little. Certainly not enough that I would pick up my towel and flee. My pleasure far exceeded any pain she could inflict.

I'm not sure what compelled me to fall across her knee. It certainly wasn't a comfortable position. With my pelvis curved around her thigh, I had to bend to the side and hold on to the wooden ledge she was sitting on if I didn't want to topple head-first onto the floor. Even so, I knew my awkward position didn't hold a candle to the terror she was about to bring down on my ass.

And, boy, did she ever!

The first spanking didn't do much damage, but the first one never does. When her hand landed down again, I realized it was still wet with my pussy juice. The third smack rang in my ears while the burn set in. She didn't seem to hold back just because she was spanking a total stranger. That woman paddled my ass like it was a sport she'd set her sights on winning, and I bore the pain well.

In any other location I would have been screaming, but I didn't want to draw attention to our activities on the off chance there was anybody out in the changing room. The cries built up in my chest until my cheeks surely glowed as red as the butch stranger's. Her spankings were too measured to be taken for angry, but they fell so hard on my ass I started to squirm. I couldn't help it. My flesh grew so raw and sensitive that every new smack saw me clawing at the wooden bench. She had to press her other hand down on the small of my back to keep me in place while she geared up for the next slap.

I found myself whimpering, "No more, no more," and crawling from her lap until my knees were on the bench beside her. When I leaned on the hot wood of the upper row, my skin sizzled. The heat of the sauna scorched my sore spanked ass.

As my butch neighbour stared at my poor red cheeks, I let my gaze wander the contours of her remarkable face. Her expression was hard to read. After bawling so relentlessly, she seemed strangely calm now. But that was always the way, wasn't it? I've endured those cries myself, sobbing until every semblance of emotion had drained from my body.

That's when I knew this was all a dream, to her. I wasn't a person, a woman, an individual in my own right. I was only a body. I was catharsis. And, you know what? I was okay with that. She obviously needed the consolation that can only come from dirty, raw sex. I could be her slut/martyr/goddess. This wasn't about me.

When she stood, I looked away, but I felt her

body behind me. I wanted to kiss her, but I knew better than to make any sudden movements.

When I felt her hot palm against the sweat beading on my lower back, my whole body went rigid. She was close. I almost jumped when her tank top met my raw ass. Even simple cotton felt rough as burlap against my sorry flesh. But that harsh sensation fell away when her fingers reamed my slit.

I was expecting *something*, but the sensation was still a shock.

She fucked me with her fingers. This was no pretty pawing. No sentimental stroking. She just plain reamed me. I couldn't even say how many fingers she shoved up my cunt. Maybe it was three. There might have been a pinky in there too, I don't know. I didn't want to turn around. I didn't want to make eye contact. It's not that I was afraid of her or anything, I just thought it might be awkward at this point. Anyway, it felt incredible, so what did I care whether it was two or three or four?

She pounded me with her fingers, and my body reacted. I banged back against her as she moved in me. Setting my forehead down on the hot wooden bench, I jerked my ass hard in her direction. She slid the hand from my back down my ass crack, and I just about jumped out of my skin.

When she spit on my asshole and shoved her thumb in there, I couldn't keep quiet any longer. Her fingers moved so impossibly fast inside me that the friction baked my cunt. I bit down on my forearm and let the ridiculous orgasm noises vibrate against my skin. I couldn't recall ever coming so hard. I lunged back at her hands as they reamed my pussy and my ass simultaneously. My tits whacked the sauna seat and sizzled each time they touched the hot wood.

The stranger didn't say anything. Not that I heard, at least, though I was making enough noise for the both of us. I didn't even care if somebody walked in at this point. What would they do, spray us with a hose? Realistically, they'd take one look at the scene of hardcore butch/femme debauchery, close the door, and walk away. Whether they'd go home and call security or masturbate in recollection really depended on the person. Either way, I wasn't afraid.

When I was spent and sore, my handsome stranger pulled her sopping fingers from my snatch and her brave thumb from my asshole. For a matter of moments, I didn't move. My chest heaved and I panted and moaned, but I didn't turn around until I felt her body shift. When I looked into her face, she quickly escaped my gaze, like she was ashamed. Like she'd done a grave injustice to the girl who'd broken her heart.

It was the most innocuous thing I could possibly have said, but I said it anyway: "It'll be okay, you know. Give it time."

She met my gaze for a split second, and then

looked to the door and nodded. As she moved her head up and down, her eyes filled with tears. Red splotches broke across her cheeks, and she quickly covered her quivering lips with the back of her hand. Before I could offer any more generic words of encouragement, she grabbed the handle, swung the door wide open, and darted out. I might have followed her if my legs hadn't turned to jelly. Instead, I climbed up on the top bench fully naked, lay down on my blazing red ass, closed my eyes, and smiled.

For weeks after the fact, every time I encountered a butch dyke on the subway or at the store or wherever, I felt my cheeks blush a little.

"Everybody knows," I kept thinking. "Everybody knows I screwed a total stranger in the sauna. One look at me, and they know what kind of girl I am."

It was like assuming the rest of the world had X-ray vision. Like every swaggering daddy on Church Street could see right through my clinging jersey dress. But maybe my coy embarrassment leant me a certain appeal, because I'd never been hit on by so many hot butch babes as I was in the weeks following that encounter.

The whole sordid experience left a lasting impression. And could it happen again? Sure it could, if the opportunity arose. Everybody knows I'm a sucker for mysterious strangers and unquelled emotion.

-5-

COULD HAVE BEEN ANY GIRL

I guess a lot of people do stupid things coming off a break-up, but I wonder how many do stupid things with strangers.

After weeks of mourning the future I'd seen in Justine's eyes, I decided the only way to feel better about myself was to fuck a total stranger. The big problem? When I got to the only lesbian club I'd ever heard of, the sidewalk was lined with bad-ass dykes. No way in hell I'd go inside.

"Hey," one of the dykes called as I turned to head home. She was big and built, but the way she flicked her cigarette to the sidewalk irritated the hell out of me. "You comin' in?"

"I don't think so." I tried to walk, but I couldn't

45

move.

She came so close I could smell the smoke on her clothes—a wrinkled shirt over compressed tits, dirty black jeans and a studded belt.

"Why not?" she asked. "You straight or something?"

Those words burned me like acid. That sneer, that smell, even her slicked-back hair made me want to punch her. And kiss her. And more.

God, why couldn't I walk away?

"If I were straight why would I be hanging around outside a pussy club?"

She sneered and said, "Maybe because you're a pussy."

Stunned, I looked to the other smokers, but their group closed off and they turned away. My heart pounded so hard I could feel it in my cunt. What if this big dyke stole me away, just threw me over her shoulder like a Viking and ran me down the street?

"I'm a pussy?" I asked when I'd regained my capacity for speech. "Does that pass for clever where you come from?"

"Do *you* pass for clever where *you* come from?" she fired back.

"What is this, Grade Three?" I couldn't believe this girl, and I certainly couldn't fathom my attraction to her. "You're just like those eight-year-old boys, where your mom says, 'He's teasing you because he likes you, honey.' It's so lame."

"If it's so lame, why is it working?" She raised an

eyebrow, too cocky for words.

I couldn't move. All I could think to say was, "Fuck you."

"I'd rather fuck *you*," she replied, like she'd prepared for this, like she was reading a script.

"Fine." What more could I say? "Go ahead."

"Fine," she said. "Maybe I will."

But she didn't do anything, just lorded over me, tall and broad and heavy.

"Well?" I prodded. "Are you gonna fuck me or aren't you? Make up your mind, because plenty of other girls would love a piece of me."

"Oh yeah?" she asked, like she'd run out of insults. "Well..."

She stood grinning, so close her chest bumped mine with every inhale. Each time her flattened breasts nudged me, a blast of juice swelled in my pussy. I wanted her fingers in there, fucking me relentlessly, unforgivingly. But she waited me out, casting smoky breaths against my face.

I didn't want to give in, but I couldn't stand the suspense. Tossing my arms around her hefty neck, I leapt against her, wrapping my legs around her waist and kissing her hard. She didn't react at all, but I didn't give up. I couldn't. I wanted what she had to give.

After a moment, she opened her mouth to mine and our tongues whipped and writhed together. She tasted like cigarettes, and that would usually have grossed me out, but not today. I needed it too badly.

Carrying me while we kissed, she backed up against the building and then turned so it was me against that callous brick. Her hands found my ass, and she ran hot palms over my bare cheeks while the wall dug into my shoulders.

Thank God I'd worn a thong, not to mention a skirt. The stranger's hands wandered unapologetically across my skin while I grinded against her belly, trying to strike my clit against her studded belt. It wasn't working.

"You gotta fuck me," I growled, crawling from her arms.

Until she glanced at the group of dykes watching us kiss, I'd nearly forgotten we were on a city street.

"What, right here?" she asked. Her voice was squeaky and high, and she cleared her throat before saying, "We got an audience, babygirl."

I didn't care. I turned around, leaned against the brick wall, and spread my legs. "Fuck me. Hard."

The dykes were all watching when my reluctant stranger shoved her hand between my thighs and shifted my thong out of the way. When the stiff night air kissed my cunt, I gasped. It felt so new to be exposed like this, out on the street before a group of gawking dykes.

The stranger took her turn with me, and the moment those thick fingers slid inside my pussy I was a helpless.

"Yeah, fuck me," I moaned, bucking back at her

hand, making her fingers move hot and fast. "Harder."

She grunted as she reamed me. Her gravel voice turned me on as much as the sloshing sound of fingers firing inside my cunt. The harder I thrust against her hand, the more forcefully she fucked me. She must have had three fingers inside, because my pussy felt full to bursting.

"Make me come!" I wasn't above begging at this point. I wanted to get off and I didn't want to wait.

"I'll make you come," she grunted. "I'll make you come so hard you'll feel it into the middle of next week."

Her words made me groan. When she wrapped one arm around my body, I knew I was a goner. She found my throbbing clit and rubbed it in quick, tight circles. I was so hot, so wet, so ready to come that her touch pushed me right over the edge.

"How's that, baby?" The stranger sneered, like she thought she'd won this game. "Tell daddy you like it."

My whole body pulsed with orgasm. I could feel it in my toes, my mind dizzy from the fall into bliss. Still, I wouldn't give that dyke the satisfaction. With my tits flush to the brick wall, I sneered, "You're not my daddy."

"Oh yeah?" Grunting, she scoured my tender clit so hard it hurt. She fucked me from behind until I couldn't stand the pleasure. I must have been whimpering, pleading, begging her to stop, because she said, "I will, babygirl. Just tell me you like it."

"I like it!" I burst. "I fucking love it, okay?"

"That's right you do." Sliding her fingers from my snatch, she slapped my ass and backed away. I leaned against the brick wall, trying to catch my breath. I couldn't remember the last time I'd come so hard. My knees went weak, and I let go, falling to the sidewalk with my skirt pulled up over my hips.

"Come on," the stranger said.

When I looked up, she and the group that had watched us fuck were heading inside the club.

"Get up, babygirl."

Nodding, I picked myself off the sidewalk, dusted a cigarette butt from my knee, and followed.

-6-
COUNTRY ROADS

Mrs. Rose called me a late bloomer because I was nineteen and still hadn't learned to drive. I had my learner's permit, but driving seemed scary. All my friends had either gone out with their parents at fifteen, or else had no inclination to drive, like me. But Mrs. Rose said I must. She drove a pick-up truck and claimed driving was the key to a woman's independence.

And Mrs. Rose was by far the most independent woman I'd ever met. My grandparents lived way out in the country, and she was their neighbour. She wasn't actually a "Mrs." at all, since she'd never been married. Mrs. Rose always told my cousins and me to call her Jan, but my grandparents were sticklers for formality and they didn't think it proper to call a woman her age "Miss" anything.

So "Mrs. Rose" it was, and Mrs. Rose she stayed.

I don't think she was actually as old as the lines around her eyes suggested. She had that colour hair where you couldn't tell if it was white or blonde, but she always wore a straw hat over it. I'd gone to her place to buy snap peas, since she sold produce to anyone who might stop by, but we got talking about driving, and soon she was set on teaching me.

Since I couldn't imagine learning in her big old pick-up, we walked back to my grandparents' property and my grandma reluctantly allowed us borrow her old-lady Toyota. Scared as I was to learn, I'd always heard it was easiest on country roads. Less traffic than in the city. Also, there was something about Mrs. Rose that made me feel safe. If we broke down or whatever, she'd know what to do.

I was so nervous when she got me to start up the engine that I thought I might pee my pants. I couldn't remember which was the gas and which was the brakes, and no matter what I did, I second-guessed myself. I felt so dumb.

But Mrs. Rose kept telling me I was doing fine. Thank goodness there was no traffic on the arrow-straight country road. I would have wet myself for sure if I saw a car coming at me.

The more I drove, the better I felt about it, until we came to a four-way stop and there were other cars there. Oh no! My legs shook so hard Mrs. Rose set one hot hand over my naked thigh, right under the hem of my short shorts.

There was a feeling that ran through me, like lightning, and all at once my nipples were so hard they hurt. The day had been so hot I hadn't worn a bra, and I stole a glance down to see if it was obvious. Oh God, it was! My nipples were pointy and thick as pencil erasers, sticking straight out through the clingy jersey of my sleeveless top.

Out of the corner of my eye, I looked to see if Mrs. Rose had noticed how hard my tits were. Would you believe she was staring right at them? Right at them! Her fingers pressed into the tan flesh of my thigh and I didn't know what to do. My pussy started to pulse, that traitor, and I told myself the impulse was purely physical, just a response to a stimulus. I couldn't possibly be sexually attracted to Mrs. Rose, with her crow's feet and sundrenched skin.

Could I?

A car behind me honked, and I started through the intersection. There was a car coming at me from the left, and I looked down at my feet, searching for the brake. Mrs. Rose grabbed my hand on the wheel, still digging her fingers into my thigh, and when she told me to floor it, I sailed through that intersection.

I kept driving, way faster than the speed limit. I wasn't even looking. I didn't care. I just wanted to get away from the car that had honked because I was so embarrassed.

But my body embarrassed me too, with its impulses, its throbbing and arousal. No matter how fast I drove, I couldn't get away from that, just like I couldn't get away from Mrs. Rose's hands on my fingers and my thigh. She was still clinging to me.

She told me to slow down and I said I wanted to stop. I started shouting at her, hyperventilating almost, as I pleaded with her to tell me how, tell me where I could pull over.

Finally, she relented and guided me into a sandy strip that looked like a driveway but didn't go anywhere. I stormed from the car because my body was full of energy, much too much. I shook it from my fingertips.

The grasses had grown high beyond our makeshift parking space, and I chopped at them with my hands.

Mrs. Rose appeared behind me. I didn't even notice her there until her hands were on my shoulders, not massaging me, but holding me steady. She told me it was all right, no harm done. I'd driven very well for my first time out. I didn't believe that for a second, but her touch reignited the pulse I'd felt before.

Turning around, I hugged Mrs. Rose and smelled the earthy aroma of her oversized linen shirt. She wore an apron in the garden, but not now. Just the shirt and capri-length khakis. When I pressed my body into hers, I could feel that she wasn't wearing a bra either. Her breasts felt soft and comforting, and an urge came over me to suckle.

I shook that idea from my head. It seemed way too weird or incestuous or something. Not that Mrs. Rose was family, but I'd known her since I was a kid and she was probably around my mother's age. Just...weird.

Holding me tight, she whispered into my ear that she'd noticed how I'd grown. I could feel her smelling my hair. *Grown how?* I wondered about that, but I didn't ask. Did she mean that we were the same height now? Or was she talking about my long tan legs, or my hips, or my breasts?

It was obvious what would happen by the way she held me, running her fingers down my back. I didn't know if I wanted it, but my body knew. My pussy throbbed so hot I was surprised it hadn't burned a hole in my shorts. My nipples felt like they'd had ice cubes pressed against them—not cold, just very, very hard.

She asked me outright if I'd ever been with another woman. I was shocked by the question, or more by the fact that she'd posed it to me in such a forthright way, but I answered. No. Never. My friend Hunter kissed me on the lips in grade seven, but that was it. Nothing salacious. Not with boys, either. Only kisses. I'd never had sex, and they called me a tease because I had a body they liked and wanted and lusted after. But they couldn't have it.

I don't think she believed I was a virgin, but why waste time convincing her? Instead, I bent my head back a little so my hair fluttered against her fingers. She still had her straw hat on, and the blazing sunlight filtered through the holes in it like slices of heaven. Her smile was bright and generous, but her eyes were dark with a lust I'd seen many times before. It followed me like a wolf, always hungry, always wanting a bite, a lick, a drop of blood.

She wanted me, and I gave myself to her.

It wasn't my mouth that she kissed, and that surprised me. She went for my neck, attacking it, nipping and licking. In moments, my knees started to tremble. There was something overpowering about her. She was slim like me, but strong. When she held my arms, I didn't struggle. I looked up at the glints of sunlight slicing through her hat, and I surrendered.

I was so turned on by the feeling of her mouth on my neck that my legs refused to hold me upright. Mrs. Rose grabbed the hem of my top and pulled it over my head as I fell to my knees. There I was, naked from the waist up, bathing in summer sunlight. I looked down at my bare breasts, and so did she. My nipples were so pink they were almost red.

There was a noise like a growl from the back of Mrs. Rose's throat, and I could feel her attraction like electricity in the air.

She set my top on the front of my grandmother's car and yanked me up by the armpits. I unbuttoned my shorts, and unzipped them without waiting for her to give the instruction. Sure I was a virgin, but I knew want—my own, and Mrs. Rose's.

When I stepped out of my flip-flops and shorts, the sunburnt grass underfoot stung my soles. I threw down my thong, which my grandmother scoffed at when she did the laundry. Mrs. Rose seemed to appreciate the look. Or maybe it was my pussy she admired. I'd shaved it the day before, because we'd gone to the beach and I wanted to wear my itty bitty bikini. Maybe Mrs. Rose would have liked me in that bathing suit. I suddenly wished I could show her. I wanted to pose for her like a pin-up model. I wanted to dance for her, and strip. I wanted to please her.

She patted my shirt on the car and told me to hop up, and I did. The sizzle of it blazed through my top, and I was glad I'd put my flip-flops back on before setting both feet on the fender.

There I was, utterly naked, pussy shaven, and sunbathing for Mrs. Rose on my grandmother's car. I opened my legs, and she dove between them.

My thighs first. She kissed all the way from my knees, down and down, starting on the other leg when she got too close to my pussy. It was such a devilish tease I wanted to smack her, but I also wanted her to tease me. I liked it. I liked that she didn't give me everything I wanted right away.

Mrs. Rose let out a wonderful noise, like a hum of enjoyment, and she told me my pussy smelled divine. She parted my shaved lips with her thumbs as I pressed my palms against the sizzling car, trying not to slide down it. When she got a look at the pink of me, she licked her lips. I could only see because her hat was sliding down the back of her head, giving me a clear view of her face. In the summer sun, her skin glowed and she looked gorgeous, more beautiful than any woman in any magazine.

I loved the way she stared at my pussy, with worship and adoration. I'd never felt so wanted. When she inched between my legs, I held my breath because I knew this was going to feel better than anything. Then she licked my pussy, really slow, teasing me still. I trembled on the hood of that car.

The day was hot, but her tongue was hotter. It blazed against my clit like liquid fire. She'd obviously done this before.

My nipples strained naked in the heat, and I wanted so badly to play with those rosy buds, but I knew the second I took my hands off the car I'd slide down and tumble to the burnt grass. So I watched Mrs. Rose through the valley of my perky breasts. I watched her eat my wet little pussy in rapture, like it was the sweetest thing she'd ever tasted in her life.

Every so often she looked up into my eyes to gauge my arousal, and sometimes she arched up high enough that I could see down the front of her oversized blouse. I saw her breasts, and they were fuller and more luscious than I'd expected. Now I really wanted to suckle them, even if that was really fucked up and crazy.

I pushed my pussy against her lips, rolling my hips to stroke my clit against her face. My straining bud had grown fat and red as a cherry. She took it in her mouth and sucked, pulling on my tender flesh with her lips. I went wild, thrashing on the hood of the Toyota. It was too much and still not enough, and I writhed so hard Mrs. Rose took hold of my thighs and held them steady as she sucked between my legs.

In the distance, I heard the approaching whoosh of a car on the country road, and I stiffened a touch. What if they saw me naked on my grandmother's car, with Mrs. Rose's head between my legs and my fat clit in her mouth? What would they think? Oh god!

I heard the vehicle whiz by, but I didn't turn in time to see it, which meant they probably didn't see us either. That's what I told myself, and the relief freed me up enough to surrender to the orgasm that had been waiting like a beast in my belly. It attacked now, and raged through my bones, making me flop about on the car like a fish out of water. I screamed and swore. Hopefully nobody heard me. I didn't think there were any houses nearby, but you never know who's out and about.

Mrs. Rose ate my cunt until I couldn't take it anymore. It felt amazing, what she was doing between my legs, but the pleasure was too extreme. It coursed through me like hot ocean waves, and that was wonderful, but her mouth on my clit was making me loopy.

She sucked, sucked, sucked until my clit felt huge and hard and tender. I screamed, and she backed away, watching my naked body come to grips with its first sexual experience.

When I was blissful and sleepy, she read my mind and unbuttoned her blouse. I eased forward and sank into the splendour of her breasts, suckling one and then the other in the teeming sunshine. Her breasts were warm and her nipples hard. I sucked them with my eyes closed, feeling heat all around me, smelling the earth on her clothes.

After she'd buttoned up and I'd dressed in my top and shorts, we sat in the hot car. We didn't do anything or say anything, just sat together until the stifling heat became too much to bear. She started up the engine and drove us back to my grandparent's place, which I was grateful for. I didn't think I was in any condition to drive after that amazing orgasm.

As she waved goodbye to my grandparents, who were sitting on the veranda of their country cottage home, Mrs. Rose offered to take me out again the next day.

I took her up on it, of course. I knew I had a lot to learn.

-7-
DILDOS AND DONUTS

Barb knew how weird I felt about sucking a fake cock.

It just seemed a little silly, getting down on my knees and licking the rubbery tip of her strap-on dildo. I did it because I knew how much it turned Barb on to watch me take that fat cockhead between my lips and imitate fellatio. It was real, to her. Not that she could feel it, but watching me suck was her favourite form of foreplay.

So I did it. For her.

"You gotta embrace the strap-on," Barb told me as she chopped carrots for the stir-fry.

I picked one up and hugged it, pretending the fat orange veggie was a dildo. "Oh, I love you so much!

Kiss, kiss, kiss."

Laughing, she grabbed it from me. "Don't play with your food, Missy."

"Well, I like when you *fuck* me with the strap-on." I started unpacking the groceries she'd left on the table. Barb had a habit of putting away anything that had to be refrigerated or frozen, and leaving the rest for me. "Actually, I love it when you fuck me with that thing, especially when you take me from behind and press those little finger vibes against my clit. Oh my God, I come so hard when you do that."

"Oh yeah?" Barb teased. "I hadn't noticed."

I rolled my eyes, reaching into Barb's shopping bag and pulling out a box of honey crullers. Those definitely weren't on the list. I held them up and asked, "Donuts?"

"Those are for later," she said.

The more I looked at the box, the more I wanted one now. "It won't spoil my appetite if I eat just one." I whined like a kid, playing with her. "Please, Mommy?"

"No," she snapped, smiling. "You be a good girl and you can have one after dinner."

Those donuts were all I could think about. Dinner was delicious, but donuts would be divine. We ate, we washed the dishes, we watched TV, but for some reason Barb kept telling me to wait. "Not yet, not yet. I'll tell you when."

Mmm... I could almost taste that honey sweetness on my tongue. I wanted a donut.

Barb turned off the TV and picked up the box of honey crullers en route to our bedroom. That's when I realized something was up. I can't believe it took me so long to clue in.

As she undressed, she said, "You know what I'd like to see you wearing? That sheer thing, like a babydoll but kind of slit down the front. You know which one I mean?"

I opened the closet and sorted through the hordes of lingerie I couldn't stop buying. It was the black babydoll she had in mind. The part that cupped my breasts had buttons at the front, but it was open down my belly, and very see-through, just like the matching g-string. I changed in the walk-in closet because I always liked to make an entrance, and when I opened the door and sprang back out, I think I was more surprised than Barb.

"There are donuts on your dildo!" I said, laughing. There were two of them wrapped like cock rings around that big black dong. It was the most hilariously alluring thing I'd ever seen.

"I know," she said. "I put them there."

"Is that what you bought them for?"

She nodded, leaning against the bed. Barb had taken off her pants but not her button-down shirt. She'd done up the harness over her underwear, and tucked her shirttails in at the sides to keep them away from the sticky donuts. What a playful mess I was about to become. I couldn't wait!

"It's finally time for dessert, huh?"

"A double dose of dessert," Barb said with a chuckle as I fell down before her.

"This is the babydoll you were talking about, right?"

The strap-on bobbed when Barb nodded wolfishly, and a nice little drizzle of honey ran down the top of the dildo, pooling when it reached the realistic cockhead.

"Oh God, I need to lick that." I couldn't resist. Leaning forward, I extended my tongue just enough to find a little droplet of honey glaze at the base of Barb's cockhead.

My senses went wild when that sugary syrup hit my tongue. Maybe it was just because I'd been looking forward to those donuts all evening, but I think I had a foodgasm. I licked circles around Barb's tip, sucking the rubbery plastic for any traces of honey.

When I looked up, Barb was gazing down at me, seeming every bit as hungry as I felt. My belly ached for sweet dough. "May I?"

Barb reached forward to press her sticky fingers to my lips, and I sucked them eagerly. Oh, I wanted sugar. I wanted more and more, and the mingling taste of her skin only added to my desire. She pushed her thumb inside my mouth, and I sucked that too, circling my tongue around and around. Her skin was delicious.

Once I'd licked every trace of sticky sweetness from her fingers, she traced them though my hair, holding my head and guiding me around the side of the dildo.

"Bite," she instructed, and I did, eagerly.

The buttery donut melted against my tongue, filling my mouth with a gush of warmth. Honey crullers were my favourite, delicate and sweet as gossamer fairy wings. I took another bite, careful only to consume the outside and leave the inner ring intact around Barb's dildo. The last thing I wanted was for my precious donuts to fall on the floor, so I cupped my hands underneath just in case.

"Now yank it down right to the tip," Barb said, guiding my head to the other side of the dildo.

I latched on to the donut, but it tore every time I tried to pull it with my teeth. They were finicky, honey crullers. It took more than a little finesse to ease the nearest one down, right down, all the way to the tip.

"Good girl," Barb said, scratching behind my ear like I was a dog. "Now eat."

I didn't need to be asked twice. Wrapping my mouth around the donut and dildo, I sucked, and the pastry melted against my tongue. When I'd swallowed every trace of that first cruller, I just kept sucking, certain I was still tasting honey in the pores of that rubberized plastic.

"Very good," Barb applauded. "Oh Missy, you look incredible sucking my big cock like that."

I gurgled, feeling at once pleased and bashful that she was watching me suck her strap-on dildo. Still, I didn't feel as weird as usual. There was a purpose to my sucking. I was driven by donuts.

"Eat the other one," Barb instructed me, tracing gentle fingers across my cheek. I shivered at the spark in her touch. I wanted so much to please her.

Arching around the side of the big black dildo, I tore into the second cruller, barely chewing before swallowing the fluffy outer layer. As before, I drew the inner ring of pastry down Barb's cock and sucked the thing until all traces of donut had disappeared.

"Keep going," she encouraged, petting my cheek as I sucked the tip. "Oh, you look so good down there. You look so beautiful, baby."

Those words anchored my arousal. When I looked up to find her gazing down at me with fire blazing in her dark eyes, I came undone. Every insecurity went out the window, and I dove at her fat cock, grabbing the still-sticky base and devouring the shaft. Her mushroom tip tickled my throat, but I wouldn't gag, not today. High on sugar and lust, I sucked my woman's fake cock as though it were real, as though the rubber were flesh and the honey was precum. I devoured her hungrily, because I wanted her to feel the love on my lips.

Squeezing her black shaft, I stroked as I sucked, but my sticky palm adhered to the dildo. Every time I shuttled my hand down the strap-on, I ended up whacking the harness against Barb's mound. She arched beside the bed, her feet sliding against the carpet, moaning incredulously with every pass.

"Yeah, Missy," she panted. "Don't stop."

Her breasts heaved under her shirt as she struggled for breath, but I just kept sucking her dick and pummelling my fist down the shaft. Barb's harness must have been rubbing or smacking against her clit—I couldn't tell which—because she issued a steady stream of appreciative curses as her eyes rolled back in her head. She thrust her hips, driving the dildo into my throat, but I didn't care. I just wanted to get her off and I knew she was close.

"Come for me," I cried around the dildo's respectable girth. "Come on, Barb! Make me eat cream."

Boston cream!

Maybe my words put her over the edge, because Barb's whole body shuddered against the side of the bed. Trance-like, she closed her eyes, shaking from head to toe.

"Oh yeah!" she cried, running her fingers through my hair, latching on and tugging. "Fuck yeah, baby. Choke on my jizz."

And I did choke, not on jizz, but on the dildo shoved halfway down my throat. My eyes watered as I gagged on her length. When Barb finally released me, I fell away from her, staring up through bleary eyes.

I'd never seen Barb so ecstatic from a blow job. It still seemed strange that she could come so hard when I wasn't even touching her, but her enjoyment made my belly glow with sweetness and warmth.

"Barb," I asked, like a child. "May I have another donut please?"

She smirked. "You can eat the whole box while I fuck you from behind."

My pussy belonged to Barb. She could have it wherever and whenever she wanted it, and I always gave myself with the greatest of joy.

Hungry for dildos and donuts, I climbed up the bedcovers and bent over.

-8-

GIRLS SLEEP WITH GIRLS

On our way to Gina's parents' cottage, we decided to pay my boyfriend Dylan's grandmother a quick visit. She was a tad traditional, he warned, but the four of us—Gina, her boyfriend Ali, plus Dylan and I—had all been crammed in the car so long we couldn't refuse a stretch. Anyway, his grandmother lived all alone and only distant neighbours looked in on her. It was a bit of a sad situation, really.

Dylan's grandmother greeted Gina, Dylan, and I with a friendly smile, tea, and cookies. Ali "the foreigner" got tea and cookies, but no smile. Classy.

As we stared out the front window in silence, the skies opened up. It poured like I'd never seen. Rain turned to hail and the steel sky turned charcoal.

"Do you think we could stay overnight?" Dylan asked his grandmother. "We hate to impose, but it's not safe to drive."

"Of course! Stay!" Grandma replied. She glared noticeably at Ali before eying all four of us. "There are two spare bedrooms. Girls sleep with girls. Boys sleep with boys. That way there's no monkey business."

We all tried not to laugh as Dylan agreed to the sleeping arrangements.

"She might even be cute if she wasn't so racist," Gina said after the matron showed us to our room. For nightwear, we could have rushed to the car in the rain for our luggage, but I had no qualms about sleeping naked.

Tossing my clothes on the floor, I slipped my bare skin under the lovely, crisp sheets.

When Gina crept into bed, her warmth spread across my skin like a wave. I'd never noticed her floral perfume before.

"Girls sleep with girls," Gina said, imitating Dylan's grandmother. "She thinks girls can't get up to no good?"

As if to challenge that belief, Gina's hand roamed to my thigh. Her fingertips felt like silk against my skin. I couldn't pretend to be surprised; it was somehow implied this would happen on holiday. The way she looked at me, I'd always known.

When I turned away from her, she didn't take it as a rebuke. She only moved in closer. Her cheek was on my hair. Her breath was on my neck. It was nearly as hot as her hand as she traced a path up my thigh.

She raked my pubic hair and I set my leg against hers, opening up. The moment her finger touched my clit, I jumped. She wrapped an arm around me, holding me in place. We didn't speak. Even as I stifled my reaction, she kept rubbing.

Gina cupped my breast, and I felt the pressure in my clit. Every part of my body seemed connected by live wires, and connected to Gina, skin on skin. I was so wet, wetter than the storm outside. Even my thighs were drenched in juice, and I wondered if Gina was equally aroused, but her front was pressed so close to my back I couldn't reach to feel. Her fingers slid around my slippery pussy lips, like she couldn't get a good hold anymore. Too damn wet. So she inched down my body, rolling me onto my back, one arm still lodged between my shoulders and the mattress.

Her breath on my nipples forced them to grow harder than I'd ever seen. They were like dark pebbles on the rounded mountains of my breasts. When she licked them, I nearly lost it. When she sucked them, I had to cover my face with a pillow. The wet heat of her mouth made me wild, forcing me to buck my hips at her hand as it circled my pussy. Then she slipped a finger inside my slit and, God, my thighs just started trembling. I was losing control, but I didn't care about the squeaks of the bedsprings as long as I wasn't shouting Gina's name to the rafters. The last thing I wanted was for this pleasure to be interrupted.

Gina forced more fingers inside my pussy, and the pressure stretched my borders in every direction. I wanted to watch her face as she did all this, watch her mouth on my tits and her fingers invading my cunt, but there was no way I was taking that pillow off my face. I was getting close, and I didn't want anyone to hear me. Anyway, there was a strange comfort in the recycled warmth of my own breath, the shallow feeling in my lungs as I gasped for air through cotton.

She fucked me with her fingers. Hard. Sometimes it hurt a little, her nails, but I was so turned on I didn't care. I rode her hand, thrusting my hips, making her fill me again and again. It wasn't like a cock. A cock couldn't fuck me this fast, couldn't slam up against me this hard.

My head was buzzing. I was biting the pillow. Gina was biting my tits. God, she didn't stop. My pussy was making all kinds of wet squelching noises as she rammed me with her fingers and I was shaking all over, loving the raw passion, and I knew she knew.

When I felt an orgasm coming on, I clenched my teeth. I didn't want to make a sound. Dylan's grandmother might hear.

Every muscle in my body tightened. Gina must have felt the pressure against her fingers, because she pulled out and stroked me so swiftly I thought she'd start a fire in my clit. A noise rose up through my body until it squealed from my throat. The pillow caught it, but not completely, and I heard Gina chuckling against my breast as she kept at my clit.

Before long, I couldn't stand any more. I tried to close my thighs, but she pushed them apart and slapped my pussy with her wet hand. Nobody had ever done that to me before. The sound of it, the sensation of being spanked on my hot pussy lips, made my clit pulse. She did it a few more times, then clenched her whole hand against my mound. My clit jumped in there, like a baby chick pecking its way out of an egg. Still, she held me like that, clutching my cunt, until my breath regulated and I pulled the pillow off my face.

Her smile was warm, satisfied, with a hint of a Cheshire grin. We breathed together for a long time, smiling, trying hard not to laugh. And when the night went quiet again, she said, "I wonder what the boys are up to."

-9-

HAPPY ENDINGS

It's kind of weird how this all came about. My assistant, Maya, asked for the afternoon off so she could participate in a documentary film. When I asked what it was about, she said *happy endings*.

I didn't know what she meant, but Maya seemed awfully embarrassed. "When I was nineteen I worked as a masseuse. It wasn't on my resume because... well, I knew what people would think."

I still didn't know what she was talking about, but I didn't ask a second time.

"Anyway, a girl I used to work with is making a documentary about happy endings. I would never give them. I thought it was gross. She wants to interview me on the con side. She's got enough girls who are pro."

"Yes, of course," I said. "Go ahead. Should be a very interesting film."

Maya grinned and called out, "Thanks, Linda," as she skipped from my office.

Happy endings? Call me naïve, but I honestly had no clue what she meant. Thank goodness for Google!

I must admit, I was a little shocked after reading the definition:

A happy ending massage culminates in sexual contact, usually manual or oral stimulation. Men are typically clients for these offerings, but some women also request happy endings. This activity is illegal in America and not performed at legitimate spas.

What kind of a place had Maya worked, if her fellow masseuses were prostituting themselves to clients? My stomach turned, thinking about sweet Maya faced with rampant erections, and men begging her to provide some relief.

At least, that was my initial impression.

As the days passed, I started looking at Maya differently. I would spot her at the coffee maker, or bent over the photocopier, and imagine those tiny hands working a stranger's oily flesh. In the beginning, I pictured her massaging fat old men, then slimmer, younger men, and then... me.

It got to the point where I could barely breathe when she entered my office. She would say, "Linda, are you okay? Your cheeks are all red."

"I'm fine," I would tell her. "Hot flashes. Just you wait!"

She'd laugh, and fetch me a glass of water. It was more than I could stand. I hadn't felt intimate touch since my cheating bastard of an ex-husband ran off with a close friend of ours. When he left me, my body shut down. I didn't want another man. I didn't want anyone, not even myself.

And suddenly, there was Maya, making me throb, making me wet. God, I wanted her to touch me, but I couldn't ask. Just couldn't. Above all else, I was a professional woman, and responsible VPs resist the temptation to seduce their staffers. I'd always believed that, and one little all-consuming crush wasn't going to sway me.

But I needed *something*. I started touching myself in the shower, but I never really got anywhere. My pussy would ache all day, and I couldn't seem to satisfy it. After a while, my brain felt like it was on fire. I became so irritated with myself that I started scratching at work, leaving red claw marks down my neck and my chest. Maya said I should see a doctor.

One day, on a whim, I asked, "How is that documentary coming along?"

She gave me a very strange look. "Weird that you'd ask. It's premiering at a little film festival next Friday. Want to come?"

"No, no." *Yes, yes!* "I don't want to cramp your style. It'll be all young people, I'm sure."

"Linda, don't say stuff like that." Maya shook her head. "Anyway, my friend wants me to invite everyone I know. She's afraid no one will show up."

"Okay," I said before Maya could change her mind. "I'll be there."

And I was there, with bells on. Okay, not bells, but my best black dress over my most slimming undergarments. I sat on my own while Maya joined her incredibly attractive young friends. The film was truly eye-opening, for me.

One woman in particular made me sit up and take notice. Her name was Shari, and she was on the pro side of the happy endings issue. "Massage represents release and relief. It's an intimate interaction, and it kicks up arousal in a lot of people. I think the natural progression is a happy ending. Touch and sexuality are so intricately interwoven. I don't want my clients leaving frustrated."

That made so much sense. Why was it okay for a masseuse to rub your back but not your front? The divide started to seem arbitrary.

After the film, there was a reception in the lobby. I'd lost track of Maya, but I spotted Shari, the eloquent advocate of happy endings. My God, was she tall! Her red velvet gown clung to her firm breasts while a black shawl draped haphazardly over her shoulders. I felt star-struck, seeing her there. My feet just started moving, and they didn't stop until I was standing right in front of her.

"Can I make an appointment?"

That's what I said. No small talk. Straight to the chase.

"Sure." As she slipped her phone from her purse, she introduced herself.

"I know," I said. "I saw you in the film."

I stared into her dungeon-dark eyes, hoping she'd know what I wanted—hoping I wouldn't have to tell her. She must have understood, because she smiled mysteriously as she looked up from her phone. "Are you busy now?"

"Now? What, you mean like right now?" I stammered like an idiot. "No, I'm free. Now is perfect."

If I'd put it off or scheduled the massage for another day, I'd surely have lost my nerve.

We slipped into a taxi and chatted about the movie. I don't even know what I was saying. I was so lost in the enormity of paying for sex. Really, that's what I was about to do.

As Shari unlocked the door of an unlit spa, she said, "We closed up for the night so everyone on staff could go to the film premiere. It'll be just the two of us."

"Oh, good."

My stomach rolled as Shari led me up a narrow staircase. I don't know what I was expecting. I just wanted it not to be sleazy. Luckily, when she opened the door at the top of the stairs, the setting sat somewhere between comfortable and clinical. I could handle that.

There was a massage table in her little room, and a fountain, some bamboo shoots, other greenery. Shari left the room while I undressed fully. I bristled with an anxious, almost embarrassed sort of heat. She knocked before coming back in the room, and by then I was flat on the prepared table, with my face through that odd pillow with the hole in the middle.

Shari gave me a whole lot of information, but my ears were buzzing. I had no idea what she said. When she set her oiled hands on my skin, I melted. It had been so long. She wouldn't have believed me if I'd told her. *Years.* So many years since I'd been touch—even like this, just her hands on my back. Without warning, I started crying.

At first, I kept it quiet. I didn't want her to hear me whimpering, but when the full-on sobs took over, I couldn't hide my sorry state. Shari asked if I'd like a tissue, and when I arched up I caught my first glimpse of her. She'd taken off her gown. What she wore now was black, like a corset with panties. She reminded me of a flamenco dancer, for some reason. She seemed wildly passionate, but totally in control.

"Thanks." I dabbed my eyes, then blew my nose. "I'm sorry about this. I don't know what's gotten into me."

"It's very common," she said. "Massage releases pent-up emotions. No need to feel sorry."

When I settled back in, with my tissues balled up in my fist, she asked if I'd like her to work her way up from my calves. Yes, I wanted that. Very much so.

When her warm palms traced oil up my legs, I melted all over again. I'd never thought of my calves as sensitive, but when Shari touched them, raw energy swirled through my pelvis. That sensation—I recognized it from years ago. From when I was a teenager, when I was in college. Long, long ago.

"That feels amazing," I said. My head was spinning, and so was my belly. My whole body felt dizzy.

Standing to one side, Shari worked her way up my thighs. The closer she got to my naked rear, the more intensely that warm energy swirled between my legs. I stared down at the floor, smiling like an idiot, and picturing Shari in her black lingerie. When she started kneading my ass cheeks, I actually groaned.

"Sorry," I said, feeling dreadfully embarrassed.

"Don't be." Her smile gleamed in her voice. "Make all the noise you like."

I wasn't shy after that. In truth, I couldn't keep it in. When she stroked my ass with scented oil, I moaned like a monster. In my entire life, I don't think anyone had ever touched me in quite that way. It felt amazing.

After a while, Shari asked, "Are you ready to flip?"

I didn't even answer her—I just did it. I turned

over on the massage table and opened my legs. Before I could stop myself, I ended up asking, "Do you ever massage people naked?"

Her lips pursed beautifully, and then she smiled. "Only if I really like them."

She must have really liked me, because she unstrung her corset and slipped out of it right before my eyes. Her body made mine pulse. I wanted to spread oil across her golden skin. Her firm breasts pointed in my direction as I stared at her bare pussy. I wished I'd shaved mine, too. I could just imagine her palm pressing against my baby-smooth cunt.

Instead, she ran her fingers through the dark curls between my legs. When I felt her slick hand against the pulpy, pounding mass of my clit, my whole body melted into the vinyl cushion. "Oh, that's good. That's sooo good."

She rubbed my pussy with the meat of her palm. I don't know if it was the oil or Shari's nudity, or just the fact that I hadn't been touched intimately in almost a decade, but my sleeping body woke up. My pussy gushed as I pressed it against her hand. She wasn't doing anything special, not that I could see, but I didn't need much convincing.

"Want me to go in?" she asked.

Her breasts surged as she rubbed me, like her whole body was doing the work. I stared at them as I tried to unpack her question. "Go in?"

She held up two fingers and raised an eyebrow.

"Oh!" When did I become such a naïve old

woman? "Yes, okay."

Shari doused my mound with oil, and just feeling that warm, slick stuff sliding over my hot folds made me moan.

When she pressed two fingers into my pussy, my bones turned to pudding. She moved slowly inside me, looking for something... and finding it.

"Oh my God!" I arched on the table. "What is that?"

"Feels good, huh?" She rubbed that strange place somewhere inside me, and I wondered if that could possibly be my G-spot. If it was... well, I finally understood what all the fuss was about.

"Thank you," I said, almost in a whisper.

Shari stroked me with her fingers, tracing gentle circles around my clit. She obviously knew what she was doing. My swollen lips felt fatter by the second. She summoned the juice that had been hibernating inside me forever. At least, it felt like forever since I'd been aroused like this, and unashamedly so.

"Don't stop," I said, gripping Shari's wrist.

From the look she gave me, I thought maybe I shouldn't have done that, but she didn't say anything, so I didn't let go.

And then she jumped and laughed and I asked, "What?"

"Didn't you feel that?" She rubbed me faster, inside and out. "Your pussy's milking my fingers. You must really like this."

My eyes fluttered. "I really do."

I didn't speak after that, not in words. I surrendered to the sensations Shari aroused in my body. It wasn't just one sensation—oh no. She made me want to push, and she made me want to pull. I bucked at her hand, launching my hips up in the air and then right back down. I wasn't in control of my actions anymore. My thighs tensed. I held my legs stiff as she scoured my clit. Then she tickled my G-spot and I nearly flipped off the table. She had to hurl her naked self on my belly to keep my in place.

"Mmm!" I shrieked and shouted, keeping my lips pressed shut. "Mmm-mm-mmm!"

My arms thrashed, and Shari jammed her tight breasts into my skin. I thrust my hips, forcing her to writhe on top of me. My brain had set itself on fire. I couldn't think. All I knew was my want—more, more, more!

The pulpy ache of my pussy expanded to devour my belly and my breasts. My eternally soft nipples drew into tight, dark buds. I reached for my breasts, cupping them, squeezing them, and that threw me well over the edge.

I wailed as the pleasure morphed into pain. Suddenly, my pussy felt huge, like a balloon set to explode. I cried, "Stop! Please! Enough!"

Shari rose from my body like a mist, withdrawing her fingers from my pussy and wiping them with a cloth. I couldn't catch my breath. My chest rose and fell. The whole room seemed hazy, like it was lost in

GISELLE RENARDE

a fog.

When Shari leaned across my thigh and blew on my clit, I shivered and laughed. It took a while to find my words, but when I did, I gushed. I must have thanked her a million times, and told her how glad I was that she'd brought me here, how grateful, how long it had been. I guaranteed that I'd make ours a standing appointment. I would come back every week—twice a week, if she'd have me.

When I ran out of breath and finally stopped talking, Shari said, "I'm glad you enjoyed it. To tell you the truth, women very rarely walk through that door. I've never given a full release massage to another woman."

She seemed like such an expert, like she knew exactly what to do. I said, "I don't believe it. You did such a fabulous job. I know I'm naïve, but there's no way that was your first time."

"Well..." Shari cocked her heat coquettishly. "My first time at work."

84

-10-
I CHASE STRAIGHT GIRLS

I read a blog post a couple weeks ago explaining "common misconceptions" about lesbians. There's only one point I remember, because it made me laugh out loud. It said straight girls are afraid of us because they're so anxious we're going to hit on them. According to the blog, that "never" happens. We dykes have expert gaydar, we know our own kind, and we never stray.

Well, let me tell you right now, that's total bullshit.

I chase straight girls all the time. I chase them almost exclusively. The more a woman insists she's not into other women, the more I want her. It's the thrill of the chase, I guess. Bathhouse and bar chicks are boring—they're so fucking easy! I can walk up to a group of pretty femmes on the dance floor, and those girls will be licking my boots by the end of the song. Where's the fun in that? Fawning femmes are neat when you're just coming out, but I've been around the block so many times my head is spinning. I like a challenge.

Lately, I've developed a taste for married women, the yummy mummy rich bitch types in particular. They're so resistant because they've got husbands and kiddies—though sometimes I think they're more concerned about what the neighbours think. Luckily, I've devised a brilliant way to slip inside these women's homes when they're alone and lonely without sparking gossip across the entire block: I started up my very own little one-woman painting business.

I figure this is pretty brilliant. See, a lot of these yoga moms have money to burn on all this home décor bullshit, but they're too lazy to paint their own damn walls. At the same time, they're not totally comfortable inviting some strange man into the house while hubby's at work and kidlets are at school. Perfect business opportunity! I posted signs all around the swanky neighbourhoods advertising the services of a trustworthy female painter. Got so many damn phone calls the first day my voicemail overflowed!

It's pretty much always the same story: I come in for the initial assessment and the quote, and they kind of cringe at the sight of me. I'm no Bettie Page, that's for damn sure, but what I lack in looks I more than make up for in confidence. And you know what? That's what straight girls are after. I come on to them in their own homes, and by the end of that first visit they're laughing at my crude jokes and writing me a cheque for paint supplies.

Last week's conquest was a prime example. Crystelle was another one of these blonde bombshell grapefruit diet types with legs to her tits and tits to her teeth. We're talking drop dead fucking gorgeous. This woman could have done porn—she certainly had the name for it, and a body to match.

So I came over to start on Project Crystelle with my paint and my tape, a drop cloth, rollers, brushes, all that jazz. She'd hired me to redo her dining room in the new season's ugly-as-shit fashion colour, and who was I to refuse? If I did a good job all around, she'd surely hire me back next year to paint it all over again.

While I covered her solid dining table and hardwood flooring with heavy cloth, she stood in the doorway watching my every move. Well, I wasn't going to waste an opportunity to flirt. I was shameless about it, in fact. What was she going to do if I got a little too crass, call my boss? So I looked that pretty woman up and down and I told her flat out that I wouldn't mind dropping her on the table and painting her naked body with my tongue.

Obviously, Madame Crystelle wasn't used to

being spoken to that way, and certainly not by the help. Her eyes blazed with an emotion that had long been familiar to me—a combination of rage, curiosity, and instant infatuation. Even though she folded her arms across her big boobs and took a step back, I knew I'd have her on that table by the end of the project. She obviously wasn't getting enough from Mister Man. I could feel that from her, like a gaping wound. The girl needed to get her pussy licked, and she needed it soon.

That first day on the job, Crystelle would go away and come back, always hovering in the doorway like a ghost, like she thought I couldn't feel her presence there. She only spoke up once, to say she was having a pot of yogurt and ask if I wanted one too. I jumped on that, telling her I loved yogurt because it reminded me of pussy: sweet and tangy, always leaves you wanting more.

Crystelle blushed and bit her bottom lip.

I asked her if she'd ever tasted pussy, and she busied herself, wiping down the kitchen counters, which were already spotless, pretending like she hadn't heard me. I asked again, and she giggled and said no, no she never had.

"Well," I said to her as I handed back my spoon and empty pot of yogurt. "If you ever get the urge, I've got a nice wet pussy that's ready just for you."

She let her hair fall in front of her face, as if she could hide how eager she was to take me up on my offer. All she said was "good to know" before turning away to wash my spoon.

When I went home that night, my muscles were aching from a long day's work, but my pussy was ten times worse. Self-denial was part of the game, when you chased straight girls. Lobster wouldn't taste as sweet if you ate it every night, would it? Same goes for women.

Second day on the job, I arrived at Crystelle's house after her husband had left for work and dropped the kids off at school. When she opened the front door, man, my eyes nearly popped out of my head! What she had on barely passed for clothes: retro short shorts, white with turquoise trim, and a tube top that barely covered her nipples. Crystelle's huge tits overshot the thing in every direction. I couldn't take my eyes off those beautiful breasts because I was so sure they were going to come flying out of that teeny tiny top at any moment.

I said something stupid like "nice outfit," and stepped by her so close I could feel her body heat through my clothes. That outfit was a sure sign she was ready for me. She must have spent the whole night imagining how it would happen. I wondered what was going through her mind as I set up for the day, pouring more paint and dipping my roller into it, spreading a slick coat against her walls. I'd primed the day before, so this was the first time she was seeing the ugly tangerine colour I was putting up. When I asked her what she thought of it, she just said it was fashionable. Her friends would be impressed.

"But what about you?" I asked. "Isn't there anything you want that's just for you?"

When Crystelle didn't answer, I knew it was time to take a risk. I set down my roller and strode across the room, but when I looked up at her, she was biting her lip, trying not to cry while her eyes got all pink and puffy.

Crying women turned me on like crazy, and when twin tears fell down her cheeks I grabbed her and held her close, kissing her hard. She made the sweetest sounds, like kittenish sobs, but I didn't let go. Pressing one hand to the small of her back, I traced the other down her ass, squeezing one cheek through those sporty-girl shorts.

At first, she didn't react. She let me kiss her, but she didn't reciprocate. Then her tongue started writhing against mine, twining and whipping in my mouth. She held my face gently, and the move was soft but it made me sizzle. I slipped both hands beneath the waistband of her shorts, and she groaned as I gripped her ass. I wasn't gentle with her. She had the choice to pull away if she wanted to, but I wasn't going to make that an easy decision.

I was the one who broke away from our kiss, but only because I knew how to make her weak in the knees. I licked her neck and she shuddered, moaning softly as she jerked her head to the side. "Oh, that feels good!"

"Yeah it does," I said, super-cocky, before sucking at her throat.

She pulled away, gasping. "No," she said in a whisper. "Don't leave any marks."

I squeezed her butt even harder, and asked, "Why not? I want you to think of me every time you look in the mirror."

Crystelle blushed and giggled, but said, "My husband…"

"You think he'll notice?" I asked, even though I knew that comment would cut close to the bone. "When was the last time he even looked at you?"

Bowing her head, she bit her lip and squeezed her eyes shut, like she could lock up those tears. I'd gone too far. See, I can read these straight women like a book and it's clear to me when their husbands have strayed, or just lost interest. Crystelle was a gorgeous woman and I told her so. When she didn't believe me, I showed her how serious my attraction was.

I told her she had great tits and I wanted to see them. Well, that obviously embarrassed her, but not enough to keep her from tugging her tube top down. Her tits sprang up like flowers in the springtime, and the fragrance of her skin struck me like a sweet perfume. She had pretty pink nipples that pursed against my cool breath. As a mother of two kids, she'd either had work done or she was insanely fit. Either way, just the sight of her made my pussy pulse. Crystelle was the kind of woman most men would follow to the ends of the earth. Me? I already had her in my grasp.

She was so tall I barely had to bend to lick her tits. Sweeping one hand to the front of her very tight shorts, I found her pussy shaved—hot and soft and so wet her juices were dripping down her thighs. No panties on this one, not even a thong! I groaned as I pressed my fingers between the folds of her blazing cunt. In my mind, I could see what a pretty pussy she had. Her mound was creamy white and her labia glistening pink. She was ready to come at my command, and I would surely take her there more than once before the day was through.

As I teased her fat clit with my fingers, I also flicked her tits with the tip of my tongue. Crystelle made it easy for me by squeezing her breasts together, so close her nipples almost touched. Her skin tasted salty and sweet, and I couldn't get enough. I lapped at her tits, side to side, sucking, even biting as she cradled them for me.

When I slipped my left hand between Crystelle's bum cheeks, she arched and yelped, "What are you doing?"

Poor woman—her husband had never tried to shove anything up her ass, and she'd never thought to ask for it. Even with me, someone she'd never have to see again once the painting was finished, she was very reluctant. Just the thought of a relative stranger prodding at her asshole made her feel awfully embarrassed. At least, that's what she claimed. I'm sure she was exhilarated as well, because when I kept right on pawing at her bum she never once told me to stop.

"Doesn't it feel good?" I asked between licks at her nipples. I circled one finger around her puckered little asshole while my other hand went crazy on her clit. "Don't you want more?"

She gave in, crying *yes, oh please more* as I sucked her nipples. Her skin was so soft against my tongue that I couldn't wait to taste the pulpy flesh of her pussy. There was nothing I loved more than eating a woman out. Girls went wild when I got between their legs. But I wanted to make Crystelle come so hard her knees gave out... then get her up on that table and make her come all over again.

I rubbed her clit in sweeping loops and her ass opened up just enough for me to press the tip of my finger inside. She groaned in a wonderfully throaty way that made me tremble, and I knew I could get her over the edge if I just kept sucking her tits, playing with her pussy, and fingering her ass.

Her pebbled nipples felt so damn good against my tongue I imagined stripping out of my overalls and rubbing them against my fat clit. But I knew that wasn't in the cards. The thing about straight girls was that they didn't know what to do with another woman. It was easy enough for Crystelle to lie back and let me pleasure her, but I didn't expected reciprocity. I wasn't that stupid.

She held my head with both hands and pressed

like a vice when she came. Crystelle was a screamer, and she obviously wasn't concerned the neighbours might hear, because she went on and on, crying out streams of pornographic curses. Her ass clamped down on my finger and her hips bucked wildly against my hand until she'd obviously had enough and pushed me away.

But I hadn't taken my fill of Crystelle, and I pushed back, urging her up on the table.

The drop sheet shifted under her bum as I pulled off her shorts and her tube top. When she was totally, beautifully naked, she spread her legs. She was still gasping for breath as I got my first look at her pussy. It might have been pink before I'd arrived that day, but after the fuss of my fingers on her clit, her labia were brilliantly red and engorged. I couldn't resist their call.

Tearing a brand new paint brush from its plastic wrap, I went to her, bending between her knees. She asked what the brush was for, but I said it was a surprise. It had a thick base brightly lacquered with shimmering blue paint. It would be perfect.

I teased her thighs with the horsehair bristles, and she laughed, but that was the least of my plan. When I got near her pussy with it, she asked if I was going to brush "down there." Her trepidation opened up the part of me that loved sparking fear in another woman's eyes, but when I teased her cunt with the bristles she just giggled. I shoved the handle up her snatch, but that was only to get it good and slathered with her pussy juice—it really wasn't thick enough to make much of an impression, as much as she cooed with delight and leaned forward to see the paintbrush jutting from her pussy.

Before removing it, I lowered my face between Crystelle's milky thighs and licked her clit. She just about climaxed the moment my tongue met her bud. It made me wonder when her husband had last pleasured her this way. Not that I was an expert on men, but it seemed to me they didn't know what they were doing when it came to clits. If they did, there wouldn't be so many married women and straight girls giving in to my advances.

I flicked Crystelle's raspberry bud with the tip of my tongue, and she grabbed my head, pressing it side to side like she'd done before. That didn't dissuade me. I licked her even harder, with the meat of my tongue now, showing her just how velvety smooth I could be. She went wild, kicking and screaming until I pulled the paintbrush from her cunt.

Her feet fell to the table and she gazed down at me beseechingly, as if to ask why I'd taken her toy. But that toy could be put to better use. I pulled hard on the drop cloth, bringing Crystelle's ass to the edge of the table. Instead of letting her feet drop, she perched her ankles up on my shoulders. She watched me wide-eyed as I pressed the tip of the paintbrush handle against her puckered asshole.

"What are you doing?" she cried, and then said, "No!"

I said *yes*, and my word was final.

Hovering between her thighs, I licked her clit with focus and power. Her asshole opened up like magic. I shoved the brush in slowly, hoping her pussy juice was enough to lubricate its path. She squirmed and squealed, but she didn't say no again, and from what I could hear while I ate her pussy, she seemed to enjoy it.

There's something special about the sight of a woman with a paintbrush shoved up her ass.

I sucked her clit and she came hard, screaming everything but my name. Her words turned into gibberish. She writhed on the table, grabbing at my hair and pulling it with those long, strong fingers. I kept at her even when she said it was too much. I pushed her limits, fucking her ass with the brush, making her come harder by the second.

When I decided she'd had enough, I backed away, leaving the paintbrush sticking out of her asshole. I liked the way it looked.

She was dazed, that was obvious. She lay there on the table as I got back to work. Whether she was sleeping or watching me, I didn't know. Eventually, she asked if I would pull the paintbrush from her ass, and I did, handing it back to her like a gift. She took it with her but left her clothes on the floor as she walked upstairs. The shower hissed and she was in there for a good long time.

When she came back down, she was dressed in pants and a long-sleeved shirt. She was cool with me, almost frigid, but that was always the way with the married ones. It didn't take long for the guilt and regret to sink in. This society programs women to feel bad about feeling good. That's just how it is.

I never expect these girls to fall in love with me, and I don't think they ever do. That's not my goal, anyway. I like being single. I like chasing straight girls. I love the thrill of the sport, but I'm more of a capture and release type hunter. They can keep their husbands and their kids and their big-ass houses and their boring sex lives. They can keep their memories, too—of that one time, that secret time, when they were seduced by a raunchy painter.

Crystelle could be cool as she liked, but she'd never forget the woman who ate her pussy on the dining room table, the woman who diddled her clit and shoved a paintbrush up her ass. And I'd never forget her either, because I had my own reward. When she left to pick up her kids from school, I shoved her wet shorts and her tight little tube top in with my gear. If I ever got lonely, I could always bring those out and give them a sniff, and remember the sweetness of a straight girl's pussy.

-11-

I HOPE WE DON'T GET CAUGHT

Judging by the number of erotic stories I've written about exhibitionism and outdoor sex, you might think I enjoy getting it on in public.

I don't.

I did when I was younger. Correction: when I was younger, I had fewer options. When I was *young* I didn't have a place of my own. I came from a large family and had little privacy. Sexual experiences were relegated by default to dry humping in a public park, or stroking in the woods, or even the odd blow job in a parked car.

Back then, of course, I was so overwhelmed by hormones I didn't give a hot damn if a dog walker, or a family of humans, or a pack of wolves passed by. The sex drive overpowered the social propriety fight-or-flight response.

That was then. This is now. This is Giselle among the grown-ups. Career, apartment, steady relationship, 2.5 cats... yup, I'm a grown-up all right. And with the security of adulthood has come the fear of getting caught.

Now, I happen to have a partner who pushes my limits. I can't even begin to tell you all the bizarre places we've had a go at each other, and yet my Sweet claims she's no exhibitionist. She has little interest in public sex. That's what she *says*, but early in our relationship she hit on this area of vulnerability for me and chose to exploit it. This, she freely admits. Nice girl, huh? But we've had a smidgen of a D/s thing going on all along, and I love the power she wields over me.

So... I've been procrastinating a bit by telling you all that. There's a story here, and I'm working myself up to it. *Giselle takes a deep breath*

Okay, I think I'm ready.

I think we got caught.

The other day Sweet had me alone. Don't ask why, but we were in church. Not at a church service or anything, just in a building that happens to be a church. My girl had been asked to open the place up for a function that was taking place there, and I was just along for the ride.

By the time we'd made the rounds, every door was not only unlocked but wide open. We were alone in the building, but our privacy was restricted by the clock ticking in our heads. People would be arriving at any moment. These impending arrivers knew us, but not as a couple. As "friends." Though I am openly and unabashedly queer, my Sweet is still very much in the closet, and I take my job of protecting her secrets very seriously.

But she's bad. Oh, that girl is bad, bad, bad. Or maybe there's just something about a church that brings out a girl's inner hussy. I really don't know. I'm not a churchgoer. In fact, I don't even know what you'd call the part of the building we were in when Sweet forced her hand between my thighs. Inside my pants, not outside. Inside my lace panties, finding my pussy wet and waiting.

There's something about my girl that keeps me eternally aroused. I'm always ready for her fingers to meander inside my underwear and part my pussy lips, rub my clit, make me come.

In that church, in the part of it where there were pews and a stage sort of area, my girl said what she always says: "I can stop if you want me to."

Oh, that vixen! Once she got her hands on me, I could never tell her to stop. Even if I'm scared to death of being caught and facing all the consequences, all the repercussions, all the embarrassment... it feels so good. Every time. And it's not just how it feels. It's a battle of wills. If I tell her to stop, she wins. Maybe I'm not such a good sub after all. Maybe I don't like to lose.

Even though we were in such an open space, clothes came off. Mine, of course. I had on a flimsy, fluttery pair of gaucho pants and she pushed them down to the floor. They pooled around my ankles, joined swiftly by my underwear. Sweet stood behind me, rubbing my clit with one hand while the other snuck underneath my top, shifting the cups of my bra, squeezing my breasts and tugging on my hard little nipples.

It never took much to make me come. I was open to orgasm any time, any place. If she wanted to take me there, I'd let her. And that day was no exception. I bit my lip to stifle the sounds of my pleasure, but my throat clicked impertinently and I whimpered, whined, moaned.

And she said, "Shhh!"

I grabbed at her arms, digging my short nails into her flesh hard enough to leave marks. Her fingers worked me harder, nudging my clit, slapping it, scouring in tight circles. As usual, it was the pressure on my tits that really set me off. All she had to do was pinch them hard and I was done.

Just as my orgasm took over, making me weak in the knees and dying to cry out, we heard the distinct sound of approaching footsteps. There were people right inside the building, in the entryway or lobby or whatever you call the place where churchgoers hang their coats. I know Sweet and I heard them at the same time because we both stopped what we were doing and righted ourselves fast. At least she was still dressed. I had to pick up my pants and pull my bra back into place.

By the time the lurkers arrived before us, I was fully clothed, yes, but looking extremely shifty.

The lurkers knew. I'm sure of it. You can tell when somebody's nervous around you by the evasive gestures and the lack of eye contact. What's worse, I'm sure at least one of those lurkers saw something, and if not *saw*, certainly *heard*. I don't know yet if those moments of questionable resolve will have consequences.

As I said, I don't like public sex. The hands tracing flesh, tearing off clothing, racing hearts, whispered words, suppressed cries...oh...oh no, I don't like it one bit.

-12-
I WATCHED HER WASH A CUCUMBER

I never would have believed it was possible if I hadn't seen it with my own eyes—and then experienced it for myself.

When I stepped out of the end stall in the washroom at work, Nazrene from Accounting was cradling a field cucumber in both hands, holding it under the faucet. The building had installed those fussy automatic sinks that never turned on when you wanted. While she tried to get the water running over her cucumber, the liquid soap dispenser spewed all over the wrist of her suit jacket. She swore under her breath, shaking it off.

"You're making a salad for lunch?" I asked.

The moment that question was out of my mouth,

I realized how strange it was that she was washing produce in the bathroom. There was a sink in the kitchen, after all.

"Hmm?" Nazrene got the water running, and rubbed the cucumber between her hands.

I stepped up to the sink next to hers, watching and wondering why she'd opted for such an unwieldy cucumber. When she caught me staring, she scowled.

Flustered, I stammered, "I haven't had one of those guys since I was a kid. The skins are tough, don't you find? I only buy the English ones now."

"Ahh." Nazrene held the field cucumber in one hand while she rubbed off the sharp little nodules with her fingers. She didn't even look up at me.

"So, I'll see you in the lunchroom?" I said, hoping to spark some reaction.

I waited for a response, but with none forthcoming I pushed the door open with my elbow and left.

Nazrene never showed up in the lunchroom that day.

She wasn't a weird girl, but she was quiet and nobody at the office knew much about her. I'd always found her pretty, in a conservative buttoned-down way, but beyond her looks I didn't think about Nazrene at all.

Not until that day I watched her wash a cucumber.

What could she have done with it? It couldn't be

what I'd convinced myself it was. Images kept flashing through my mind of Nazrene taking that giant cucumber into a bathroom stall, hiking up her skirt, throwing down her panties, and fucking herself silly. Is that really what she'd done?

You know what they say: the most obvious answer is usually the right one.

About a week later, I stepped out of the washroom stall to once again find Nazrene at the sink. Just like before, she had a field cucumber between her palms and she was rubbing it under running water.

I watched her wash it, mesmerized by the motion of her golden brown skin against the cucumber's deep green flesh. Her rings glided up and down her wet fingers as she rubbed the thick, long vegetable. My knees went so weak I had to lean my hip against the sink to keep from keeling over.

"Will I see you in the lunchroom?" I asked. My voice was a whisper. I could barely hear myself, so I wasn't surprised when Nazrene didn't answer.

When I left the bathroom, she was all I could think about.

The third time this happened, I was bold enough to ask, "What's with the cucumber?"

She looked up at me, looked straight into my eyes, and said, "I'm going to the roof."

"The roof?" I wondered if that was any kind of answer to my question. "Isn't it locked? I didn't know we could get up there."

"The lock's broken. I'm going up." She tugged a few paper towels from the dispenser and dried off her cucumber.

I couldn't stop staring at the thing. I couldn't figure out what was going on, if she was inviting me up, if she was actually going to eat that thing, or if she would do what I kept picturing.

"Can I come too?" I asked.

Nazrene shrugged, and that was good enough. My lunch was in the fridge, but I could forego a meal if it meant discovering the fate of that big cucumber.

Following Nazrene up six flights of stairs, I watched as she pushed the roof door open with her hip and stepped out into the gleaming sunlight. Shading my eyes, I walked out after her.

To my surprise, there was a garden on the roof with a few small trees and hardy rushes. I walked past them, away from door, and meandered along a path to the soft little flowers that grew close to the ground. I couldn't resist bending to stroke their downy petals.

"Pretty, aren't they?" Nazrene smiled when I looked up at her. She eased her long body down into the patch, cucumber in hand.

Though I had my suspicions, I asked, "What do you do up here?"

She never stopped smiling. In fact, she beamed so intensely I started to back away a bit. It wasn't until she raised the cucumber to her lips and kissed the end of it, grinning like the devil, that I halted. What could I do? I just stared at her, my jaw slack.

Nazrene raised her eyebrow—only one, not the other—and I knew it was an invitation. Maybe it was the heat of the sun or the altitude, or even just the softness of the flowers under my bare knees, but I wanted her. I wanted everything she wanted, and maybe even more.

Leaning back on one elbow, Nazrene opened her legs, drawing her business-length skirt up past her hips. I gasped when I saw that she wasn't wearing any underwear. Her pubic hair was black but very trim, and I couldn't take my eyes off the glimmer of juice coating her pussy lips. I watched in amazement as they opened to reveal the perfect pink glistening inside her labia.

Right away, there was a thick pulse between my legs. It beat so forcefully I would have touched myself if Nazrene hadn't been there staring at me.

I didn't think I could speak, but the words tumbled out of my mouth hot as lava: "Put it in."

Nazrene tilted her head, smirking. Then she extended the cucumber in my direction and said, "You do it."

I grabbed the thing from her. There was a part of me that wanted to ram it up her snatch just to see how she'd react, but I knew she'd put her trust in me. I knew she had faith. So I was gentle. I took it slow.

I'll never forget the way Nazrene's pussy lips

glistened as I traced the domed end of that cucumber around them in sweeping circles. Every time I got to the top, I nudged her clit a few times and she opened her legs even wider, bucking her hips off the ground. Tossing her head back, she hummed her approval like a song, and the sound of her voice like that, full of longing and desire, turned me on more than I ever could have imagined.

My palm was sweating so much it was hard to keep a firm hold on the cucumber. It was just so massive I didn't know if it would really fit inside her. I had to pull the big vegetable away just to get one more look at that tight little hole. Her slit was deep pink bordering on red, and that wet flesh seemed to be grasping for the pleasure I'd taken away.

"Put it in. Put it in!"

Nazrene's voice was thin, and it cracked when she begged. The sound made my pussy clench, just like hers was doing as I watched, and I ached to spread those engorged lips. I wanted to use my fingers, or even my fist. I wanted to drill inside her with my body.

"Put it in," she repeated, again and again, like a mantra. Her eyes were closed now, her head tossed back, lips slightly parted. Her long black hair swept the groundcover, shimmering in the brilliant sunshine. "Please."

I couldn't resist any longer. Pressing the tip of the cucumber flush to her slit, I pushed with enough force to make her yelp.

"Sorry!" I cried. "Did I hurt you? I'm so sorry!"

She raised her hips and her head simultaneously, glaring at me for a good beat before offering an impish smile.

"Keep going," she said, and I did, twisting the cucumber as I went. Every time I turned the thing one way or the other, Nazrene writhed along with it. Her breasts rose up in the air and, God, they were gorgeous—so full and round. I could smell the tang of her cunt overlaying the aroma of garden flowers as I forced the cucumber inside her, watching her pussy open to a big O.

How could something so tight accommodate something so big? It seemed impossible. I'd never been penetrated by anything so huge, and I didn't want to be. Big cocks scared the hell out of me, and this cucumber had a greater girth than any flesh-and-blood man in existence.

Even so, I felt strangely empowered as I held that thing in my hand. Jamming it into Nazrene's beautiful cunt, I felt like a superhero.

Not roughly, mind. The last thing I wanted to do was hurt her. Nazrene had opened herself up to me in the most intimate way imaginable. She'd stretched my boundaries, and all I wanted to do was fill her with pleasure. For me, I knew that would involve more than just ramming a cucumber in my pussy. For me, it would take some clit stimulation.

I wondered if Nazrene was anything like me. I

wondered if she'd like what I liked, but I didn't wonder for long.

Leaning forward, I breathed in the musk of Nazrene's cunt. Now that my fingernails had pierced the cucumber's flesh, I could smell its freshness so much that I was salivating wildly as I plunged my face against her crotch.

With her pussy lips spread wide, all I could do was plant myself above her clit and lick that tender bud. The cucumber was filling her now—I could tell by the resistance her cunt muscles exerted as I pressed forward—so I used the lust she'd inspired to lick her like crazy. I don't think my tongue had ever flicked so fast. Nazrene went wild, hollering as she dug her hands into the groundcover, sending up earthy scents of soil and grass.

She looked like a totally different person this way. Around the office, Nazrene was so buttoned down, so put together. Now she was a wild woman, crying out, "More, yes my lovely, more!"

I gave her what I could, licking her little clit like crazy, hoping that was enough. Her screams caught somewhere between exultation and torment. How could I leave her hanging?

And then her hand was in my hair, twisting it into a rope, pulling, yanking, hurting me. I didn't care. Her insistence only made me work harder, and the better I did, the more I gave, the more her pussy clenched around the cucumber, making it jerk in my hand.

Bucking her hips, she fucked the massive vegetable, grinding her clit against my tongue, getting off on both at once. The cucumber whacked my chin, but what could I do? Nazrene wasn't saying words—only screaming, crying, yelling out nonsense syllables while she thrust her hips.

Her excitement made my heart race, and I licked her as fast as my tongue would let me. My jaw ached, but I couldn't stop. I wouldn't quit until she told me to.

And that came soon enough. Nazrene bucked high up off the ground, teeth clenched, squealing through them, fists balled in my hair. I tried to move the cucumber in her cunt, but she was just too tight. No matter how much I licked her clit she didn't loosen up.

"No!" she cried, which was the opposite of what I was used to hearing in bed. "No more! Too much, no more."

I looked up at her, and her eyes were wide as dinner plates, like her orgasm had put her in shock.

"Careful," she warned as I pulled the cucumber from her pussy.

She smelled so good, like salad and musk. I wanted to eat her in every way possible.

Nazrene held that pose, leaning back in the bed of flowers as I held her cucumber. She watched me like I'd watched her when she was washing it—with an expression of sheer intrigue.

And then she said, "Lick it, my lovely."

God, the way she looked at me when she said those words... how could I refuse? I'd somehow managed to ignore my own arousal while I got Nazrene off, but now that she was spent and sore I wanted my turn. If I licked her cucumber, would she lick my pussy? I certainly hoped so.

I hadn't gotten the full taste of my beautiful co-worker's cunt just by flicking her clit with my tongue. When I took a long, languorous lick of the vegetable, the taste of Nazrene hit me full on. It had a sweetness to it, as well as the brightness from the cucumber's spritz, but it was the dense musky aroma of pussy that really stuck in my throat. I turned the thick vegetable in my hand, lapping up every trace of pussy juice.

By the time I'd finished, the cucumber shone with saliva and my throat was thick with the taste of Nazrene.

"Your turn," she said with a sly grin.

I smiled. "You want to eat my pussy?"

"No." She gave me a curious look and then glanced at her beloved cucumber. "I want to fuck it with that."

My stomach knotted as I looked between Nazrene and the giant cucumber. "What? No way."

She nodded slowly and then snatched the cucumber away from me. "Yes!"

"No," I said, though I'm sure she could tell I was fidgeting to hike my short skirt up and over my hips.

"On your knees," she instructed, like her word was final. "I'm going to fuck you from behind."

I just sat there staring for what felt like forever. My heart pounded so hard I felt it in my cunt. I couldn't think of any reason to resist her... or the cucumber.

Pulling my slick panties down to my knees, I bent over so my ass was in the air and my forehead touched the soft groundcover. I could feel my whole body cringing as I waited for Nazrene to make her move.

She pushed up my skirt to get it out of the way, and then rubbed my ass cheeks with her palm. When I thought about her staring at my asshole, I felt so humiliated my brain started to buzz. This was all so... weird!

And then suddenly—smack!—she slapped my slick pussy lips with that big green monster. I rolled my head enough that I could watch from underneath while she smacked me again. Boy, it made me shiver when the cucumber drew a gossamer strand of nectar from my snatch. In the bright sunlight, my pussy juice actually shimmered.

"Fuck me," I groaned, though the idea of that huge vegetable filling my pussy still made my stomach clench. "But go slow. Don't hurt me."

She said nothing as the cucumber's rounded tip met my slit. I thought it would be cold, but it wasn't. Being inside Nazrene's pussy must have softened it up, because when she started pushing it into me it didn't feel quite as huge as I thought it would. Not that it wasn't gigantic, but I really thought it would hurt.

"Play with yourself," Nazrene instructed. "Touch your clit, my lovely."

My bud was so engorged I actually gasped when I touched it. I couldn't keep still. I arched off the ground.

"Stay," Nazrene commanded, pressing down on my lower back. Her hand was so hot I wouldn't have been surprised if it left a brand on my flesh.

I could feel the cucumber pulsing in my cunt, opening me wide, and I tried not to think of what Nazrene's pussy had looked like when I'd forced that same veggie into it. I couldn't imagine being stretched that wide. I couldn't believe it was happening to me.

Rubbing my clit, I said, "More! Give me more!"

My pussy was unbelievably sensitive: my lips were thick and my clit throbbed, begging for release. Nazrene put more pressure on the cucumber and I felt its smooth curves opening me wider. My fingers whacked the monster as I scoured my bud, lifting one shoulder and crushing my cheek into the soft ground. I wished I could open my blouse to feel the soft flowers and grasses caressing my naked nipples, but my breasts were pressing down too hard. Anyway, I was too turned on to be coordinated.

That's when Nazrene started twisting the cucumber inside my cunt, just like I'd done to her. It entered me deeply, and it felt so foreign, so unusual, so unabashedly huge that I wasn't sure how I could handle its girth.

"Come for me," Nazrene chanted as she turned the cucumber. "Come, my lovely."

She juiced me like an orange, and it felt so oddly wonderful that I knew I'd find my orgasm if I just kept stroking.

I was right.

Shocks erupted through my belly, streaming down to my tits, exploding like fireworks. I lost all control at that point. Without fear or reservation, I bucked back. Nazrene held steady, driving the mammoth cucumber into my pussy as my orgasm took over.

Up on the rooftop, I grunted like an animal, like I wasn't human anymore. "Awww yeah, fuck yeah fuck yeah fuck yeah!"

My voice was gravel. I didn't recognize it, except that it resonated in my chest like a canon blast. When I squeezed my eyes shut, galaxies exploded against the darkness of my lids. My skin was on fire, and that fire blazed through me until the only sensation left was the stretch and pull of a massive cucumber lodged in my snatch.

I lost track of time until Nazrene carefully slid the monster out of me. My pussy ached for it, but I knew I couldn't bear any more. I'd be feeling my distension for a week.

Nazrene stretched out beside me and licked my

pussy juice from the cucumber's dark green skin. It was quite a spectacle, and my clit started pounding again as I watched her. I was just about to touch it when she said, "Back to work. We're late already."

A deep flush consumed me when I saw the grass stains across the front of my blouse. How was I going to explain that away around the office? My heart started thumping again, and my knees went so weak I didn't think I'd be able to stand, until Nazrene helped me to my feet.

Before edging into the dark stairwell, Nazrene shielded her eyes from the sun and asked, "Would you do it again?"

My pussy was swollen and sore, I had grass stains on my boobs, and my panties were soaked. Any sensible woman would say no, but the word stuck in my throat and before I knew it I'd said, "Any time."

On our way downstairs, I asked Nazrene, "What are you going to do with that cucumber?"

She held it tight and said, "Slice it up, add some tomatoes, red onion, Greek dressing—makes a nice salad. I'll bring some for lunch tomorrow, if you'll share it with me."

What could I say? "Yes, please."

My mouth was watering already.

-13-

MY GIRLFRIEND THE SEX DREAM PSYCHIC

I'm convinced my girlfriend knows when I'm about to cheat on her in my sleep.

Yesterday morning, Desta had work in the city, so we planned to go out for a late lunch and then back to my place for..."dessert," as they say.

Now, one thing you should know about me is that I keep very odd hours. I don't usually go to bed until four in the morning at the earliest, and I'll often sleep until noon. Bad, bad habit, but my body seems to like it.

Of course, my girlfriend knows how I operate. Yesterday, she was smart enough to give me a wake-up call. Here's what I can remember of the dream she interrupted:

I'm some kind of CSI-type investigator person and I'm working alongside the young guy from *Without a Trace* (I don't remember his name). We're smooshed into a car as we check out evidence inside it. Cramped quarters. Bodies pressed tight together, shoulder to shoulder. We're discussing the case but the sexual tension is out of this world. We turn our heads and I know it, I can feel it... we're about to kiss...

Ring ring ring ring ring!

God damn it! The phone was ringing just as we were getting to the good stuff! I tossed off the covers and stumbled to the cordless, grumbling, "Hello?"

"Just wanted to make sure you're awake," Desta said in that super-sweet voice of hers. It was almost like she knew what she was doing. "Don't forget lunch, okay?"

Hearing Desta's voice always makes me instantly happy, but I was still a little curious how that dream would play out. So I didn't get up. Rebellious little devil that I am, I went back to bed.

I dreamed, but it was a different dream this time:

There's a girl. I don't know who she is, but she's hot: darkish skin, darkish hair, jeans and a black tank top...and massive breasts. She's in my apartment, for some reason—in the kitchen. She's talking about her long distance relationship, but I'm so focused on those gorgeous tits that I'm not really paying attention. I cling to her like a koala bear, wrapping my arms around her neck and my legs around her waist. She carries me over to the couch and I nuzzle my face into the curve of her neck. What would she do if I copped a feel? I think she'd be okay with it, but I'm super-nervous. I'm going to do it. I'm going to touch those big, beautiful breasts. I'm just going to run my hand down her chest and...

Ring ring ring ring ring!

Oh, you have got to be kidding me! I fell out of bed, hobbled across the bedroom, and grabbed the phone. "Hello?"

"Did you go back to sleep?"

"Nnnn...yes?"

Desta knows me too well. "You missed lunch."

What? What time was it? How long had I been asleep?

Just as I started to apologize, somebody knocked at the door. With the phone in hand, I ran to see who it was, and there she stood. "Desta!"

Storming into my apartment, she swept me off my feet, crushing my mouth with fierce, fiery kisses. Just like in my dream of the big-breasted woman, she pressed her chest against mine, squeezing me breathless with her powerful arms. My girl had it all: strength, beauty, and the boobs of my dreams.

"Nice dress," she said, tugging at my satin chemise. "Take it off. I want you naked."

Tossing me on the couch, Desta ripped off her clothes. When I was totally nude and she had on nothing but a tight white undershirt and a pair of navy blue boyshorts, she dove between my legs. Holding my ankles wide apart, she attacked my pussy, licking my clit with perfect precision.

"Oh Des!" I ran my hands through her hair, loosening her ponytail until her long locks tumbled against my thighs. "God, I love your mouth!"

She growled as she sucked my clit between her lips. I watched her face between my thighs, bobbing and gulping, and it looked and even felt like she was giving me a blowjob. The very idea of ramming a huge erection down my girlfriend's throat sent me into sensory overload.

I grabbed both my nipples and twisted them so hard it hurt. The pain danced down my body, finding my clit and exploding in Desta's hot mouth. I tried to move on her tongue, but she had to firm a grip on my ankles. I was stuck like that until she elected to let me go.

Not yet. She kept at me, slowly now, licking up and down my slit as our gazes locked. Desta always looked so hot like that—mid-lick, fleshy pink tongue extended, tousled hair sticking to her cheeks, eyes dark with lust. If I had a picture of her looking just like that, I'd frame it and put it on the table beside my bed.

Finding my hole hot and wet, Desta made her tongue hard like a cock and pierced me with it. That wasn't something she normally did, and the sensation was queer to me. Unfamiliar. She fucked me with her tongue, and her mouth suddenly seemed much bigger than usual. Her plump lips closed around my mound like a vacuum pump, and somehow she was sucking me and fucking me at once.

Her hands held my ankles so wide apart my legs formed a straight line, but her fingers also traced a path up my quivering belly. They found my nipples and pinched tight as little crabs, making it hurt so sweetly my body rippled and writhed.

"I'm gonna come again, baby." My words were like steam, evaporating into the open sky. Somehow it was night-time again, and we were on top of a train, feeling its locomotion rumbling through our bodies, making my full breasts jiggle as I exploded with orgasm.

Ring ring ring ring ring!

I looked down at Desta in utter confusion, searching for the phone, asking, "Where is it? How do I answer?"

Ring ring ring ring ring!

That's when the light from between my curtains struck me in the face, and I realized I'd been sleeping again. This had all been a dream.

Rolling out of bed, I answered the phone. I shouldn't have been surprised that it was Desta.

"You fall asleep again?" she asked.

I laughed, glancing up at the clock. I hadn't been out all that long. "You know me too well."

"Get up and get dressed," she said. The sizzle in

her voice made my pussy feel hot and heavy. "And meet me at the restaurant *on time*. No excuses."

"Yes ma'am," I replied before saying goodbye.

Bed was tempting, but I didn't go back. If my dream Desta could make me come twice in as many minutes, who knows what my real life Desta had in store?

-14-
NAILED

Mandy never used to hold my hand in the car. This was new, this one hand on the wheel, one pressed into my palm thing. I loved the innocent romance of it. Handholding was Betty and Veronica, complete with the love triangle. Ours was an all-female version, equally contentious, and focused entirely around big, beautiful Mandy.

Pink polish. Her fingernails were glossy, but they shimmered purple in the blue light from the dashboard. Every time we hit a bump in the road, they dug into the meat of my hand. It hurt so good.

But if I thought my kitten had claws in the car, that was nothing compared to the bedroom. Her daggers really came out when we got to my place. I brought out my thickest strap-on dildo and she dug those treacherous nails into my ass so hard I screamed.

She knew just how I liked my pain.

"God, that hurts." I wrapped my legs around hers and held her in my arms. "Feels incredible. But it hurts."

"Thought so."

"I love it, Mandy." I growled like a bear, bucked like a bull, until my dildo couldn't take the heat and popped right out of her pussy.

I slowed my thrusts, guiding that slippery shaft back inside her unfathomable wetness. After that, I fucked Mandy gently enough to stay inside. Cocks had minds of their own. Even fake ones.

She writhed beneath me, pushing her big tits against mine so our nipples played and pressed together. When kissed, she dug her nails into my flesh and squeezed. My body leapt and I gasped like pain was my oxygen.

"Too much?" she asked, teasing, knowing very well it wasn't.

"No, baby, feels good." I hugged her body tight, forcing my fake cock up inside her. The strap stroked my clit with every thrust, but there was a part of me that wished I could feel her pussy muscles clamping down on my dildo. If only there were artificial nerve endings I could hook up to feel that pressure.

Mandy's fingernails closed the sensation gap, and

she must have known it.

"More," I pleaded. "Make it sore."

I wanted to feel the hurt all week. I wanted to feel it on the days she spent with Aisha instead of me. When I was alone in bed, wondering if Mandy was alone too—but too afraid to call and find out—I wanted to feel the sting of my girl's fingernails, a reminder that she loved me too. The pain would serve as a memento of our lust.

But Mandy teased me, tracing her nails up my back so lightly it tickled, making me shiver as I shoved my cock in her.

"Harder," I begged.

"I don't want to hurt you," she said, always teasing, taunting, dancing her fingernails across my skin.

"I *want* you to hurt me." I thrust in her, making her whimper and cringe and tighten the muscles in her thighs.

She hesitated, tracing her fingers down my ass, gently, too gently.

"It's not like anyone's going to see the marks," I said—a loaded statement, and she knew it. I could tell by the look in her eyes.

Exclusivity.

I'd tried not to push too hard, but she knew I wanted exactly what I offered. I wanted her to be mine and mine alone, just like I was hers. *Exclusively.* There was no other girl I wanted. Just Mandy. Why couldn't she be satisfied with just me?

The smile on Mandy's face did it. I bubbled from the inside out, kissing her cheeks, her nose, her lips as I rocked inside her. She dug her nails into my ass and I arched away from her mouth. Gasping, I cobra-posed on top of her full body and cried out, "Oh God!"

It hurt like hell, but I loved it. She was right about me. She was totally right.

"Sometimes I look at you," I said, "and my insides just feel like they're gonna come bubbling out."

She rolled her eyes like she didn't believe me, so I fucked her harder, sliding one hand around her front. Slipping it between our sweat-soaked bodies, I found her clit. Her eyelids fluttered closed as she arched. The sight of her like that, so close to ecstasy, made me want to stop everything and take a picture.

Then Mandy scratched ten red lines into my ass, and the sheer sting of it moved my hips in double time.

"I look at you, Mandy..." I grunted as I fucked her. "I look at you and my temperature rises. And then you touch me and I'm so hot I can't stand it."

She squinted, squealed, threw herself at my strap-on. "When you get hot, I get hot."

"Yeah?" I asked, grinding against the harness, getting myself off on the strap while she writhed beneath me.

"Oh yeah, baby."

Mandy dug those lacquered nails into my fleshy

ass. My body heaved itself against hers. My hips went crazy. I knew I could get myself off like this. I was just about there. We could come together. We could do it.

"How hot are you now?" she asked, panting, her voice thin as linen.

"So fucking hot!" I growled.

Her razor nails dipped down the small of my back, slicing a path to my shoulders. The pain egged me on like a brand. I fucked her so hard she screamed, finding my ass once again and driving her nails into my flesh.

"You really like this, don't you?" She was laughing and panting at once.

There were no words to express how much I loved her nails. I loved the sharp stabs and lingering sizzle, so I kissed her, melting and melding into her mouth.

She tore me to shreds as we came together. The flood and gush of our orgasm took everything from me. All the energy I'd had was suddenly gone, and my thighs ached. We were drenched in sweat, panting, straining, drained.

I pulled out, letting my cock rest on her thigh as I lay on my side. Staring. God, she was beautiful with her hair stuck to her temples. She was so beautiful I could die.

My back shrieked with pain and I could just imagine how it would feel when I took a shower—the soap, the sting, the hot needling water. For some reason, that made me think about Aisha, and my mood dropped down into hell.

Mandy must have read my face, because she sighed. I thought I knew what she'd say: "Don't start," or maybe, "Just be happy we're together right now."

But I was wrong.

She said, "You know I love you."

"I know. I love you too." I kissed her chest, her shoulders, eager to show her just how much. I sucked her breasts, and for a moment she was quiet.

Then she said, "Aisha. I love her too."

I pulled away from Mandy's nipple and nodded. My bottom lip quivered, and I bit it until my mouth filled with the metallic sting of blood.

"But she's so jealous now," Mandy went on. "She never used to be. In the beginning, she was mature about our situation—like you are."

Usually, I didn't like hearing about Aisha, but hope swelled my heart. Did Mandy mean... was it over between them?

"I had to walk away," she said, and I felt the weight of her heartbreak in my chest. "Jealousy is relationship poison, and once it's in your veins that's the beginning of the end."

For the first time, I really understood how much Mandy loved both Aisha and me. I'd secretly painted our open relationship with a much blacker brush than it deserved. All this time, Mandy was full of love for us, but Aisha and I were too competitive to see each other's worth.

My back and my butt stung from Mandy's nails, but I couldn't enjoy the sensation just yet. Now that I had exactly what I *thought* I wanted, I realized I wanted more.

"You've got so much love to give," I told Mandy. "And you know what? So do I."

She looked at me and smiled like she knew just what I was going to say next.

"Let's talk to Aisha." I'd usually feel embarrassed to suggest it, but the marks Mandy left on my skin had opened me up to new possibilities. "Let's do more than talk."

"That's what you want?" Mandy asked, leaning up on her elbows.

I nodded. "If she wants it, I want it too. We could be good together, all three of us."

Mandy leaned in to kiss me softly, and then she whispered, "Aisha's got nails like the devil. You're going to love her, babe."

-15-

ON THE SEVENTH DAY

Nobody told me yoga could be habit-forming. Then again, nobody told me anything about yoga at all. I discovered it in the wee small hours of the morning, when I was flipping through TV channels trying to put off the inevitable chore of going to bed.

Insomnia had crept up on me so slowly I didn't immediately recognize it. Soon, I was tossing and turning for a good three hours before falling into a light sleep that never seemed to last. When I saw that yoga program on TV, I knew instinctively that it would be my salvation. Every night after that, I tuned in, did the entire routine with the pretty instructor, and then went to bed.

Finally, I could sleep again! Yoga was better than

any drug.

There was one problem, though: the yoga program was only on six days a week. On Sundays, it was replaced with some GED training show, which I'm sure was very helpful to some people, but it didn't manage to put me to sleep. I still hadn't learned enough poses to make up my own routines, so Saturday night into Sunday morning I'd lie awake waiting for sleep to take over. After six days of perfect rest, a night of tossing and turning just wouldn't do.

There was only one other way I knew to expend energy. It wasn't something I did all the time, but that seventh day, the day without yoga, called for drastic measures.

I went to my drawer of naughty treasures and pulled out all three of my vibrators—mama, papa, and baby. I grabbed the lube as well, because I knew I'd be needing that miracle elixir. Wearing my skimpy silky nightie, I grabbed a towel and laid it over the bed. I'd just changed my sheets, and I knew this could get messy.

Kneeling over the towel, I hiked up my shorty nightie, but the texture was so satiny and slick that it slipped right back down. I pulled it up again and trapped the hem between my chin and chest, which forced me to gaze down at my pubic hair. It seemed darker and thicker, more unruly than it had been even the day before. I stared at it, trying to catch sight of my clit in the moonlight. No trace of pink, not from that angle. As I turned on mama vibe, all I could see was the dark hair curled across my slit.

Maybe it sounds weirdly incestuous to refer to sex toys as mama, papa, and baby. It would be better if I categorized them by colour, or texture, or size. The baby vibe was obviously the smallest. It was a cheapie made of slick purple plastic, super-reliable and perfect for ass play. In fact, that's all I used that one for.

Papa was my big daddy vibe: generous girth, low and slow vibrations, a gripping black monster just perfect for my pussy. But the one I got the most use out of was the mama, the medium-sized toy, not too hard, not too soft, sturdy, but with just enough give. That one was light blue and ribbed, so when I stroked my clit, its vein-like bumps gave me even more sensation. Not that I needed it with the blue vibe—it was the most powerful thing I owned, like a motorcycle with a supple sheath.

Squirting my hot pussy with cool lube, I pressed the blue vibe to my clit. The vibration was so extreme I arched back, curving my spine until my tits were sticking straight up and my head nearly touched my toes. I guess that yoga was really paying off. I'd never been this flexible before.

I turned down the juice and started again. My nightie fell against my belly, and I couldn't see my pussy at all anymore, but that wasn't the end of the world. I stroked my clit, letting the ribs tease my wet little bud, building my arousal slowly after that immediate jolt I'd just given myself. It felt good to climb that mountain to orgasm. I didn't mind taking my time.

As I rubbed my go-to vibe against my aching clit, my pussy gaped jealously. Time for the big daddy dildo. My cunt was already so sopping wet I didn't even have to reach for the lube. Kneeling up a little higher off the bed, I slipped the black cock beneath my body and lowered myself until the fat tip sat against my slit. I inched the vibrations up a tiny bit higher on the blue vibe, then sank down, letting my pussy devour the monster dildo.

When the big cock panged at the upper limit of my cunt, I held steady, reaching down to turn the toy on. It was older than the rest, and it rumbled loud and low, like a thug groaning while he fucked me. I doubt I'd ever seek out a flesh-and-blood man to bed, but in my secret heart I imagined all sorts of scenarios: all bodies, all genders, all types of play, and even a little yoga. In my mind, anything could happen.

Edging my feet inward, I held the big guy between my heels. I started riding it, slow and steady at the start, building up speed as I scoured my clit with the blue vibe.

I always liked to watch my boobs bounce while I fucked a dildo, so I pulled down the straps on my nightie, letting my hefty tits spill over the top. My muscles worked overtime as I rubbed myself off with my trusty vibe, but I knew the tension would be worth it. My mattress squeaked as I bounced on my toy, increasing the vibration with my feet and feeling the buzz fill my pelvis.

"That's so good," I kept chanting, hoping I wouldn't wake the neighbours. But who knows? There was always a chance I might summon that perky yuppy who lived down the hall—the one with the bouncy orange curls and the coffee cup glued to her hand. Maybe, if I made enough noise, she'd storm into my bedroom, grab my big daddy, and fuck the life out of me. Imagine that! Being taken in every position imaginable until I collapsed in bed and slept for a hundred years. Maybe I should scream even louder.

I came hard on two vibes, one on my clit and the other filling my snatch, but a single orgasm was never enough, even if it was a really good one. Letting the monster vibe chug away inside my pussy, I rested my clit and took a few slow breaths. It felt nice to fill my lungs and regulate my breathing, so I closed my eyes for a few minutes, letting the black toy's low vibrations take over my clit and my ass.

Without opening my eyes, I reached for the smallest toy and held it between my clenched thighs as I drizzled it with lube. I grabbed it by the base and turned it on. The purple guy didn't have the most powerful vibrations in the world, but my ass was super-sensitive. Anything would do.

Holding the little purple vibe in place with the

pads of my feet, I lowered my body until its rounded tip rested against my asshole. My butt could be finicky about what got shoved in it, so I never forced anything. I sat there, kneeling on my towel, one huge vibe lodged firmly in my cunt while a much smaller one waited to enter my ass. And then I touched the blue mama to my clit.

I gasped at the overwhelming sensation. Vibrators everywhere! It was enough to get my asshole to open up just a bit, allowing the slim plastic vibe inside, little by little. The harder I scoured my clit, the more my ass opened up, but it wasn't happening as fast as I wanted. I've never been particularly patient, and I forced my ass down on the mattress, throwing caution to the wind.

Big mistake, as always. My ass screamed in pain, and I jerked up from the bed, bringing all three vibes with me. My pussy and my asshole were strong enough to keep those toys in place, but only for a moment. When they both started to slide, I plunged back down on the mattress, forcing them farther inside my body.

Fuck, it hurt—especially my ass—but I'd gone too far to stop now. I wanted another orgasm, and I wasn't above chasing it round in circles half the night. Luckily, it didn't take long. I turned my clit vibe up to full power and it put me right over the edge. The vibrations were so powerful I wanted to steal them away from my clit, but I forced myself to keep it there.

My newly-flexible yoga back arched, and I held my almost-upside-down pose as I scoured my clit. Throwing myself upright, I fucked my two vibes hard, feeling the black one filling my pussy as the purple one destroyed my ass. There were slices of pain along with the pleasure, and those incongruous feelings brought me deeper and higher than I'd ever been before.

I fucked my toys hard, nearly swallowing them whole before I couldn't stand any more of that raw sensation. When I pulled them out and turned them off, the relief was fleeting. My asshole stung, and my pussy felt bruised outside and in. But I was too relaxed to worry.

Maybe tomorrow's yoga routine would focus on healing fresh sex wounds.

In seven days, I'd be ready for another round with three vibes.

-16-
RING OF ROSES

I spent three hours crying in her bed.

She was right there, snoring beside me, but I couldn't get past the gnawing sensation that she'd never be mine, not entirely. Her house was full of meaningful knick-knacks and mementoes, little reminders of a marriage that, in my mind, would never cease to exist. Was there really room for me?

There were photographs everywhere, in every room. Why so goddamn many photographs? Why did I have to look at them? Or, better yet, why couldn't I see past them? *I'm the girl who's sleeping in her bed, the girl she chats with every night, the girl she pulls into the shower with her, and that's all that matters.* I tried to comfort myself with those thoughts, but I guess I savoured my sadness too much. There were certain things neither of us would release—Danielle had her pictures, I had my pain.

Danielle had told me many times that I was being juvenile. I knew she was right, but I could never reconcile my emotions. "I don't know why you let things get to you," she often said. "Let my actions speak for me."

But I only saw her inactions. I only saw the photographs still hanging on the wall.

That's why I booked the couples' package in Niagara Falls, complete with king-size bed, in-room Jacuzzi tub, and a dozen red roses. We still had a few more days we'd committed to spending together, and I just couldn't stand another night in her bed, haunted by those all-too-real pictures of a ghost marriage. Instead, I would whisk my girl off on a surprise getaway for two. Perfect.

I guess I could have told this story as a sickly sweet romance with me as the gallant sugar mama. It still would have been objectively true, but it wouldn't have been the complete and unadulterated truth. If I'm going for honesty I might as well go all the way, even if the reality makes me seem immature and a little bit crazy.

You should have seen her face when I announced the trip. I'd never seen her so ecstatic. She rushed to fetch her suitcase and I sat on the bed while she rifled through her closet, holding outfits up against her body. "I wonder if this still fits... Oooh, a cleavage dress!"

For the first time since I'd arrived at this house I was never comfortable in, I felt happy and hopeful. Danielle's joy gave me that gift.

"Where are you taking me for dinner?" she asked.

"The Brazilian steakhouse."

Her eyes lit up. "That place is expensive!"

Everything was expensive, but there was only one perfect response to that statement: "Anything for my girl."

We arrived in Niagara just after noon and took a walk by the Falls. The weather was mild for January in Canada. Cottonball snowflakes melted as they hit the pavement. When the breeze turned cool, I led my girlfriend the amateur photographer to the horticultural centre so she could practice her hobby on bright tropical plants.

This whole trip might have been spur of the moment, but I knew Danielle well enough to plot adventures she would appreciate. Her happiness was truly my greatest joy, though she'd probably tell you my greatest joy was getting laid. Maybe we were both right.

When we went back to the hotel to dress for dinner, Danielle admired the blood-red roses I'd organized for the room. I wanted to be the only person in the world who'd ever bought her roses, and it was a strange source of anguish that I couldn't change the past to make that true. I wanted to. I wanted to wipe out her history, but all I could do was give her roses and steak dinners and jewellery and hotel stays, and hope to one day supersede everything that came before me.

If I hadn't already.

I threw on the best outfit I'd brought and then sat on the ledge of the Jacuzzi tub, watching my girlfriend meticulously applying her makeup. I felt like a kid again. It was like watching my mother get ready for her office Christmas party, back in the day. The dusty rose scent of loose powder brought back a lost sort of magic.

Danielle put on a necklace I hadn't bought her, and I hated how much that irked me. Wasn't it enough that she was wearing not one but two rings I'd given her? Did I need to dress her like a child, pick out jewels from among those I'd purchased? Hell, maybe I could just own her outright and keep her in a cage. Then I'd never have to feel jealous.

The woman I loved had a past. I needed to accept that, or we'd fall apart. I could feel us tearing at the seams already.

"Well?" she asked, doing a little turn. "How do I look?"

I'd told her a hundred times she was the most beautiful woman I'd ever met, but she never took my compliments to heart. In that low-cut black dress, she took my breath away. I didn't even get a chance to plant my face between her boobs before she was reaching around me for her coat, saying, "Come on! We're already late for dinner."

Dinner! Now that she was dressed to the nines, all I wanted to eat was her.

But Brazilian steak was a close second. The meal was delicious and the setting romantic beyond belief. Our conversations had that giddy early-relationship feel, where you're fascinated by everything your date has to say. I couldn't stop smiling, and she rolled her eyes and grinned every time my gaze dipped down into her cleavage.

After dinner, we took a leisurely walk through the nearby casino, and then headed out into the night, gripping each other tightly as we descended the slippery slope toward the Falls. We arrived fallside just in time for the nine o'clock fireworks—a happy accident, which Danielle caught on film while I snuggled up against her.

Everything was perfect. Everything. I kept waiting for something to go wrong, and then telling myself to keep the negativity at bay. *Just let this weekend be wonderful. Enjoy Danielle's company. Don't ruin it.*

After we'd walked back to the hotel and let our toes defrost, Danielle took off her makeup while I filled the large Jacuzzi tub. When the water level looked about right, I broke apart two long-stemmed roses and scattered the petals across our king-size bed and over the gently steaming surface of our bath.

It was, by far, the most conventionally romantic thing I'd ever done, and even though Danielle and I always claimed to spurn convention, I think we both enjoyed the ambiance those blood-red petals added to our room.

"Too bad we didn't bring any candles," I said as I stepped into the tub. "Would have been romantic."

I laughed when Danielle asked, "Should I join you?"

"I hope so! I didn't book a Jacuzzi suite so I could sit in here alone while you watched Letterman."

She stepped in, grinning. The tub was perfect for two, with enough space not to feel cramped and yet not so much that we were distanced from each other. My legs pressed against her side, and hers against mine. Red rose petals swirled around our bodies in figure eights while we gazed at each other, waiting for something to happen, wondering who should make the first move and what that move should be.

"Should we turn on the jets?" I asked, though the question sounded stupid even to my ears.

"Sure," Danielle said, like she was just happy to be along for the ride.

I pressed the button and the jets came to life, blasting me from every direction. The rose petals danced along the water's surface, some diving and bobbing, others finding my skin and latching on. I took one of the satiny petals and traced it along my sweetheart's jaw line, then down her neck and across her shoulder.

"You have the smoothest skin I've ever touched." I felt it under the water, playing with her toes and making her squeal, padding my fingers up her calves as she inhaled deeply. "I love your legs, especially in heels."

"Especially in black thigh-highs." She'd worn them that evening, all black lingerie because she knew what I liked.

"Crap!" I said, squeezing her thigh. "We didn't take any pictures of us together, dressed for dinner."

"Oh well," she said simply. "Next time."

Would you believe I was still thinking about her walls back home? I wanted to see myself inside those frames—wanted to see *us* there. Was I crazy? I had to be, if I was going to let something so stupid ruin what had so far been the most beautiful day of our life together.

So I dove at my girlfriend's naked body, taking her freshly washed face in my hands and kissing her mouth. She never believed me when I said her perfect cherubic lips looked better without lipstick than with, but it was true. They were eternally plump, rosy red, gorgeous, and when they opened for my tongue I was ruthless.

The evening's pulpy romance came to a head in that moment. She hugged me hard, returning my kisses as I pressed my naked body against hers. There was nothing better than feeling warm and wet all over while velvety petals hopped and danced against our skin. And, though we were hardly afraid of the light, we usually made love in relative darkness. It was refreshing to get a good look at my girl's ample curves—the ones she referred to as "fat."

She touched my skin, brushing one hand down my ass while we consumed each other with kisses. Everything that led up to this moment kept playing though my mind: walking in the snow, pictures in the greenhouse, the sheer romance of dinner for two, and then fireworks over the Falls. This was the absolute perfect ending to an absolutely perfect day.

I didn't notice at first that Danielle was sliding against the side of the tub. It didn't occur to me that we were sinking until her my nose met the water. When Danielle's face was completely submerged, panic struck. I struggled to right myself.

We scrambled against the sides of the tub, laughing, no worse for the near drowning and, best of all, covered in rose petals.

"Are you trying to kill me?" she asked, giggling as she wiped water from her eyes.

"Why would I? It's not like I'd get anything out of it. I'm not even named in your will."

I shouldn't have made that joke. It made me think about things I preferred to ignore—like the legal rights we lacked because we weren't married, we didn't live together. *The photographs.* Every damn thing led back to them.

No sense being sad on vacation. I put on a smile and turned in the tub, tossing my feet across the ledge. "I'm just going to get myself off on this jet. You can do whatever you want over there."

More teasing, and she knew it.

"Okay, fine," she said melodramatically. "Just ignore your girlfriend. You don't care about me anyway."

"Ha!" Sometimes I thought I cared too much about her, like she was my addiction. Anyway, Danielle was a total voyeur when it came to my pleasure. She loved watching me get off on my hand or my toys, or whatever did the trick—and this tub surely qualified.

Jacuzzi jets were new to us, but I knew how much she would love watching that blasting stream of water gush against my pussy. Grabbing hold of the little nozzle, I jerked it around and arched when the jet struck my clit.

I turned to Danielle and saw my amazement reflected in the expression on her face. "Wow," she said, with a visible shudder of excitement. "That looks good."

I loved her ability to sense my arousal vicariously, to actually feel my pleasure in her body. She was like some sort of sexual psychic.

"It feels amazing!" I closed my thighs for a moment and reached for one of the jet nozzles close to her, adjusting it to blast between her legs. "You should try."

"I'm happier watching you," she said, which wasn't unusual. Sometimes Danielle wasn't keen on direct stimulation, whether it was my touch or a jet spray, but we'd been together long enough that I didn't take her occasional stoniness personally. After all, I enjoyed sensation enough for the both of us.

My breasts bobbed just above the water's burbling surface. My nipples were hard as pebbles. Rose petals kissed my bare skin like scarlet lips, and I took hold of one, smoothing it down my sweetheart's neck and chest, pressing it flush to one nipple and then the other.

Danielle's breath grew shallow. I could feel its pace quicken with each rise and fall of her chest. When I looked into her eyes, I met the familiar darkness of her lust.

"Open your legs," she said, reaching for my thigh. "Let me play with your pussy."

I smirked, adjusting my position, wanting the jet to find my clit again. "You just love my pussy, don't you?"

"Mmm-hmm!"

"You even love it when I said the word 'pussy.'"

Her eyes gleamed with knowing desire as she spread my lips with her fingers. I'd shaved for her, and being bare made my pussy even more sensitive than usual.

I gasped when the jet found my clit. "Oh my God, Danielle."

"It's good, huh?" That sneaky grin turned me on as much as her naked body surrounded by a bustling ring of rose petals. I reached between her thighs, stroking there, and she said, "What if I do

146

this?"

Holding my pussy lips open with her index and ring fingers, she rubbed my clit with her middle finger and while the jet pummelled my pussy. Her touch felt so good I couldn't keep myself from bucking out of the water. Even when I arched high out of the tub, she didn't stop stroking me.

God, was she good with her hands...

My clit was already aching and engorged from the jet. Danielle launched me over the edge. It never took her long to make me come, but paired with a Jacuzzi jet, she got me off at record speed. Everything she did, whether it involved her fingers or her tongue or whatever else, got me so worked up I couldn't contain myself. I always said it was my attraction to her that lit the fire. Her touch made me burn.

Danielle pushed my body underwater, aligning my clit with the jet. Once she had me where she wanted me, she grabbed the nozzle and turned it in circles so it struck my throbbing clit.

I splashed carelessly, and she grabbed my breast to settle me down. But once I got going, nothing could keep me from seeking out the next orgasm, and I begged her to pinch my nipple.

"Like this?" She squeezed my tit between her thumb and forefinger.

"Yes!" I cried as a lightning bolt shot from my nipple to my clit. "Do the other one."

"Like this?" she asked again, twisting my other tit

so hard it hurt.

"Yes, yes, yes!" I thrust my full weight against the Jacuzzi's stalwart blast, bringing a wave of water and rose petals with me. The wave crashed against the side of the tub and I let it carry me back, astounded by how light I felt in the hands of this warm bath.

In the midst of so much pleasure, I hadn't paid much attention to my girl's sweet body. I pressed my hand between her thighs, stroking while she pinched my tits and pressed a finger into my pussy. I kept waiting for her to react, to give some sign that my touch was making an impression. After a while I accepted that she wasn't keen that evening and set my hand on her thigh, squeezing gently while she pushed another finger inside me.

"Oh, that's good," I moaned when she went for three. It was a tight fit, but I was so aching and aroused I just wanted more, more, more. I fucked her fingers and the Jacuzzi jet while she filled me and stretched me. Still, the warm gush pounded my clit. It felt harder all the time, like the more turned on I got, the more pressure it blasted me with.

Now it was Danielle's turn to pick up a rose petal and brush it across my skin. It felt so lovely, so velvety soft against my cheek that I slowed my thrusts to concentrate on that beautiful sensation.

When I looked up at my girlfriend, the downy expression on her face made me breathe deeply. "You really are the most beautiful woman in the world," I told her.

I figured she would brush off my compliment as flattery, but when she blushed and said, "Thanks," I wondered if I'd finally convinced her it was true.

When Danielle dragged a rose petal down my chest and then across my tortured tits, the sensation brought a swell of buzzing heat to my pelvis. I felt another orgasm sitting right there, so close to the surface I could almost taste it.

My sweetheart knew just what to do. While she fucked me with her fingers, she bent down and flicked one nipple with the tip of her tongue.

"Oh God," I groaned, knowing I was right on the edge. "Yeah baby, suck it."

She moved to the other breast and teased that nipple with her tongue. Even with her lips parted, I could see the grin on her face.

"Suck it!" I begged her, pressing the back of her head against my breast.

She turned to look at me, pressing her cheek against my nipple. Her fingers hadn't let up—they were still fucking me impossibly hard, never slowing, though her knuckles rapped against the tub with every blow.

I was so close, so close. The other orgasms were just prep work, just baby orgasms leading up to the mother of all. I bucked against her fingers and the Jacuzzi jet, because those were the key ingredients, but I knew the second she sucked my tit I would come so hard she'd feel it vicariously.

Bathwater and rose petals lapped against Danielle's face as she watched me flirt with this orgasm. "You want me to suck your tits?" she teased.

"Yes!"

Without answering, she turned her head softly. I wasn't sure if it was the sight, the sensation, or just the build-up, but when Danielle wrapped her lips around my nipple, the buzzing weight in my pelvis erupted. The release was like a shimmering heat blasting through my core, warming my heart and body together. I was screaming, moaning, whimpering as Danielle nibbled my tits…

And then the Jacuzzi timer tick-tick-ticked above my head and, all at once, the jets turned off.

Before the rose petals could stop dancing in the water, I cried, "Turn it on! Turn it on!" and Danielle reached her one unoccupied hand up to bring the wicked tub back to life.

The very second that jet blasted my clit, I soared back into climax, this time higher than before, feeling the heat rising, swelling, releasing through my clit. I looked past Danielle's beautiful face to her hand pounding my pussy while the invisible power of the jet made my lips dance like the petals. I was so turned on my clit was nearly same colour as those roses. I knew I couldn't take much more. There was a thin line between pleasure and pain, and I was starting to feel the internal itch that meant pain was close at hand.

My pussy muscles were still milking Danielle's fingers when I crossed that threshold, crying, "Enough, enough! No more, babe."

But she didn't back off, not right away. She swooped me away from the abrasive jet, but replaced it with her thumb, rubbing my clit in circles—hard.

I squirmed and splashed in the tub, screaming now, crying under that heavy sense of "I can't take it anymore" until she kissed me quiet.

Slowly, she eased her fingers out of my pussy. Rose-infused bathwater soothed the aching heat between my legs as we writhed together, kissing gently, flesh against flesh.

"Your skin is so soft," I said, though I'd said those words many time before. "I love it. I love the curve at your side, where you rise and fall, where your hips give way to your thighs." I kissed her shoulder and she kissed my neck. "I love your legs. I love your feet. I love your toes. I love *you*."

"I love you too," she whispered, like she was in a daze. We turned off the jets and rested together inside a ring of rose petals until out fingers were pruny. And then we got out and dried each other with fluffy white towels.

Danielle turned on the TV, and when I joined her in a bed strewn with rose petals, she was watching Letterman and eating jujubes. There was something impossibly cute about that, and when I snuggled against her bath-warm body, my heart felt too big for my chest. I wanted this feeling—always. No more juvenile insecurities. They'd plagued me from the very start of our relationship, but I was getting tired of being jealous of a memory. We were together, in bed, in love, in life. It was time to grow up. It was well past that time.

Naked and happy, I kissed my girl and she tasted like candy. "Did you have fun in the bath?" I asked.

"You have no idea," she said with a little laugh. "You'll never believe how much pleasure I get from watching you come. It's better than feeling it myself."

"It's better to give than to receive," I replied—that was her motto.

"Exactly," she said, and when I scooped a handful of scarlet petals off the duvet, she took a deep breath and blew them across our bed. My chest filled with warmth as I watched them flutter and fall.

-17-
SAUCY CHEEKS

I looked for the blaze in Donna's eyes, but I only found loving amusement.

"I'm so sorry I'm late!" I said. "This snooty bitch wouldn't leave my department at closing time. I had to call security! Then I wait forty minutes for the damn bus and, of course, three come at once..."

Donna cocked her head in the direction of two look-alike dykes I was meeting for the first time. That was the whole point of this dinner, actually: to get to know some of Donna's friends. Great first impression I made, showing up late like that, but the women seemed amenable. They introduced themselves, but I immediately forgot who was who. They were strikingly similar in appearance: heavy-set, short sandy hair, dark clothes, lots of piercings.

"Nice to finally meet you." I slouched into the chair they'd saved for me. "Sorry again for being…" I glanced at my phone and my chest tightened. "Oh God, I'm over an hour late!"

"We had to start without you," Donna said with a smile. "In fact, dessert's on the way."

"I'm really sorry," I repeated, seeking some recognizable response.

Donna set a hand on mine. "Don't worry about it. You're off the hook."

The other women laughed, and one said, "Until you get home!"

I felt a blush cross my cheeks. *How did they know?* Did Donna discuss our private life with other people? The thought made me uneasy, and I squirmed in my chair.

When I didn't say anything, Donna's friends started talking about a movie they'd seen, and I was glad the focus had shifted. What did these women know? Was nothing sacred? I shivered, and Donna must have noticed, because she wrapped her white pashmina around my shoulders.

Donna's friends were still talking, but I shot my girl a look that asked, "Are you sure? You know I'm messy."

She nodded, and I absorbed the warmth of my woman through the fabric. When coffee and cake came, I sat a little taller. I'd been nervous on the way there, but that chocolate mousse slice drizzled in raspberry coulis made my mouth water.

"Can I have some?" I asked Donna.

"We ordered two slices," the woman on the left clarified. "One for each couple."

"Aww...that's sweet." I smiled as the women kissed, and nearly jumped out of my chair when I felt Donna's lips on my cheek.

Donna had never kissed me in public. She'd never even held my hand! This was... new. And wonderful! I felt all warm and fuzzy as I sipped coffee with my girlfriend's pashmina draped around my shoulders and folded across my chest.

And then it happened: I took a forkful of mousse cake, lifted it to my mouth, and watched in slow motion as a drip of red coulis slipped through the prongs of the fork, beading against the soft fabric. *It'll be okay*, I told myself, but as I wiped up the droplet, the cake itself tumbled down. It broke into layers of cake, mousse, and deep chocolate icing. Oh God, that would never come out...

"I'm sorry," I said for the fourth time in the space of five minutes. "I am such a klutz. I'll try to wash it."

"Maybe ask the server for some soda water?" one of Donna's friends said, but my head was buzzing too much to process the advice. I stood, flicking the cake to the plate and removing my girl's pashmina.

"I'll come with you." Donna pushed her chair back and rose from the table. "I'm sure we can get it out."

155

I never felt so small as when I'd done something wrong. I walked to the washroom in a daze, feeling the hot press of Donna's front against my back, but never turning to acknowledge it.

"I'm sorry," I said again, when we'd passed through the bathroom door.

Before I knew it, Donna's mouth was slanted across mine, our lips a tight seal. This never happened. *Never.* But it was happening now—Donna was kissing me in a public bathroom, and kissing me hard! I couldn't get over the heat coming off my girl's body. I felt consumed by it.

"I thought I'd be in trouble," I whispered, panting with arousal.

Donna tossed the pashmina in the sink. "Who says you're not?"

The growl in her voice and made me loopy. I couldn't believe it when Donna yanked me into the end stall—the big one.

"Pull down those pants," Donna instructed, even before the stall was closed.

I did as I was told, dropping my slacks and cotton underpants to the floor. I didn't mean to get myself in so much trouble.

Sitting fully clothed onto the toilet seat, Donna patted her lap and I fell into it. At home, this was standard practice, but we were in public...well, in a public washroom.

When the top of my head met the toilet paper dispenser, I used it as leverage to turn around and watch. "I'm sorry I was so late."

"You're off the hook, remember?" Donna's eyes were uncharacteristically kind as she spoke. "Now, the pashmina...that's another story."

"I'm sorry about that, too." My pussy clenched as I awaited sweet punishment. "If I can't get the stain out, I'll buy you a new one."

Donna seemed to time her "Thank you" exactly with the first smack on my ass. I let out a little yelp, hoping there were no other patrons in the washroom. We hadn't even checked.

"How many?" I asked as the second slap fell.

Another one—three so soon, and all in the same spot. "How many do you think?"

"Ten," I said without reflection.

I knew I'd want more.

Four came down hard in that same tender spot, and I couldn't contain my squeal. Lower for five—that one came down around my thigh. Six did, too—other cheek, other thigh.

I allowed my body to be shifted in Donna's lap, like I was on a Lazy Susan.

"Harder," I begged.

"Harder?" Donna asked, with surprise in her voice.

"Please?"

Harder is exactly what I got for seven, eight, nine. They fell like rapid fire, in quick succession, and they were solid spankings every one of them. I hissed, but I wanted more, oh so much more!

Ten was a disappointment: off the mark, falling in the middle of my ass crack without connecting properly.

"Bonus round?" I pleaded.

"Saucy Cheeks!" Donna never denied me a bonus round.

The next one was much more precise than the last. It caught the burn of my right cheek, and I watched my flesh ripple before settling down.

Switch for the next one. It came down hard on my left cheek, and the sound was like the crack of a whip. I squealed, and my feet ran along the floor as I anticipated the following spanking.

The next one was more than one. They alternated, rapid fire, one, two, one, two, back and forth across my burning bottom. The pleasure-pain crossed the threshold to pain-pain, and I couldn't stop myself from crying out, from saying, "Ow...it hurts!"

My skin sizzled when Donna decided the punishment was complete. My bum burned so badly I couldn't put my panties on right away.

Donna left the stall for a moment, and came back with her pashmina, wetted with cold water. Again, she folded me over her lap. This time she soothed the burn, tracing soft, cool wetness across my poor searing bottom. It was an act of such love and compassion I wanted to cry.

After a time, we left the stall and stood together at the sink, trying to rinse the chocolate and raspberry stain from that beautiful white scarf. I jumped when one of our dinner companions poked her head in the door and handed us a glass of soda water. "Hope this does the trick," she said, and promptly scuttled away.

I met my girl's gaze in the mirror and smiled. "Thanks for setting this up," I said. "I like your friends."

"You hardly met them," Donna replied.

"Yeah." I turned to her and winked. "But they sure know me."

-18-
SIGHT OF MY WOMAN

How would I get through another night alone? My girl Monique was still away at her Ottawa conference, and I was proud as hell of her success…but I was horny as hell, too.

Lifting the picture frame from my bedside table, I dove into Monique's loving eyes. "God, girl, do you have any idea what I'd do to you if you were here right now?"

Her gaze was so innocent. She had no idea what was coming. I would have to phone yet again to tell her.

"I've been waiting for your booty call," she said, throaty and low, like she was ready for me.

"Are you in the mood?" I wasn't wasting any

time.

She burbled with sensual delight. "Oh yeah, Jackie baby, just lying naked in my big hotel bed and thinking of you."

The image made me moan. "Mmm... I wish I could take you, throw you down and kiss you."

"Kiss me where?" she asked.

"Kiss your neck, for starters."

"Then what?"

I closed my eyes and imagined it. "Lick you and suck you. I would love that right now."

"Ohhhh yes." She cooed like a dove, and I could picture her rosebud lips forming an endless O. "That would be wonderful. I feel a tingle just hearing you talk about it."

"You're tingling? I love that."

I could hear the smile in her silence.

"I know how much you enjoy it when I get between your thighs and I take your little clit in my mouth and reach up to play with your boobs. When I take you in my hands and squeeze... God, you've got lots to play with."

Monique went quiet, waiting for more. I could feel her eagerness through the phone line.

"If you were here right now, I'd stare at your nice pretty pussy because, wow, just the sight of it turns me on. I'd press my fingers inside your wet slit and it would be sooooo sensitive because only you and I have ever touched there. I'd dip my fingers in and pet inside your pussy, right at the front where your g-spot is, and you'd feel pressure almost like you have to pee. You'd feel warm and tingly as I rubbed you there."

Her throat clicked and I knew she must be playing with herself when she said, "Mmmmm."

"I can feel your pussy grasping at my fingers. It's hot and wet and it just wants, wants, wants. Your pussy lips are getting big and red and all engorged with your arousal, so I lean in and I lick your clit, just a little teasing lick."

"Yesss…" A hiss, a slight moan. Monique was getting off on my words.

"And you sigh and you want more, oh so much more. You're quiet and you don't beg me for it, but I know…"

"You always know."

I smiled into the phone. "So I keep petting you on the inside, and I lick your clit. I lick it hard and I suck it and I lick it again and now you're so turned on that you mash your pussy against my mouth and you make me take it, and your pussy gets my lips and my chin soooooooo wet."

"So wet…" She was breathing hard, and I could have sworn I heard her wet fingers working at her sweet cunt, bringing her closer and closer.

I wanted to put Monique over the edge. "Baby, you come so hard from rubbing your clit against my tongue that you can't help being loud and crying out and moaning because it just feels sooooo good."

"Mmmmm…" Yes, she was definitely getting off

in her big hotel bed, with my voice helping her along.

"And if you tell me to stop because it's just too much," I asked, "do you think I would stop?"

"No, don't stop!" she cried, which was about the most I'd gotten out of her this entire phone call. "I want more. Keep going. Pet my pussy. Lick my clit."

"You coming, over there?" Stupid question.

Monique squealed into the receiver, and I gazed at her photograph while she wailed. The glass over her picture was all smudged from my kisses. I kissed everything that reminded me of her—the photo, the phone, the bedpost. She made me wild, and my heart threatened to burst every time I thought about her.

"I miss you," I said when her cries calmed down.

"We're still together," she consoled me. "Even if you're there and I'm here. Plus, I'm coming home soon."

I smiled and sighed, like I always did when our conversations were coming to a close. "I love being in love with you, Monique."

She laughed, and I could tell she was embarrassed, like she didn't deserve all the affection I felt for her. "You're too sweet, babe. Too sweet."

Even after we'd said goodbye, I couldn't be sure I wouldn't call her again. But after I hung up the phone, I stared at its face in my moonlit bedroom and I kissed it gently. I kissed my girl goodnight.

-19-

SOUND OF MY WOMAN

"I want you, Monique."

"You are so sweet," she said into the phone. "And so hot."

"You're hotter." I wasn't sure if I was leading this phone sex session or just trying to keep up. Monique always expected me to know what to say, like it was easy. "I wish I were licking your pussy right now."

"Do you?"

"Oh yeah." I pictured her up in Ottawa, all alone in that stark hotel room, and the words just came to me. "I want to get my face between your thighs and just wreck you. I want to lick you until you scream."

"God, yes…"

"And then lick you some more."

"Mmm..." Monique purred like a kitten. "You devil. Where did you learn that from?"

"From the best," I said, to make her feel good. "I want to tear you apart, babygirl. I want to gnaw at your clit. I want to eat you so hard you have bruises the next day, so every time you ache you think of me."

"God, you are in *need*!" she chuckled.

"Am I turning you on, you little vixen?"

"You're definitely getting a reaction." There was a distinct blush in her voice, and I wondered if she was stroking her clit like I was stroking mine—just casually, playing with the possibility of rubbing it harder.

"I want you so badly," I told her. "I want to suck your nipples. I want to trace my tongue along your tits."

"You are *horny* tonight!" Her breath was shallow. She must be touching herself too.

"I am *so* horny, babygirl." I liked talking this way. We never did it when we were together, in the same room. We never talked like this in bed.

Maybe it wasn't such a bad thing, Monique being away from me for a few days. It gave us space to want each other.

"Are you horny too?" I asked her.

She didn't answer, except with a whimper, but that was just her bashfulness. I knew she wanted me as much as I wanted her.

"Are you playing with your pussy, babe? I'm

playing with mine." I stroked my clit harder now, with three firm fingers. "God, my cunt is so fucking juicy right now. You wouldn't believe how wet I am."

"Me too," she said, breathlessly.

"Yeah?" I smacked my wet cunt and it felt so good I did it again. "Did you hear that babe?"

"No." Her words were distant, like she was a world away. "Hear what?"

Holding the phone near my pussy, I spanked myself so hard it made me jump. "That."

"Oh God." Her breath came faster. "What was that?"

"I slapped my pussy for you."

"Oh Jackie!" Her voice was tight now, strained, like she was close and just needed me to push her over the edge. She chuckled again and I could tell I was making her nervous. Sometimes I was so intense it shocked her. She asked, "Would you slap my pussy if I was there?"

"Fuck yes."

Monique gasped.

"Do it to yourself," I dared her. "Spank your wet cunt, baby. Do it now."

I didn't hear the slap, but I did hear her hiss and then gasp, and that's how I knew she'd done it.

"You liked that, didn't you?"

"Yes," she said, drawing out the s-sound. "Oh, yes."

"Are you going to do it again?"

"Yes."

I heard the slaps this time. Maybe she'd moved the phone closer to her pussy like I'd done for her. The smacking sounds came down fast and furious, and all I could picture were her pretty fingernails painted the same colour pink as her glistening pussy lips. My Monique was so damn beautiful.

"God, I wish you were here right now."

"I don't think I'd survive if I were," she said.

"Oh, I'd keep you going," I assured her. "Because I want to kiss your neck, kiss your tits, kiss your belly. I want to kiss you everywhere."

"Are you ever thirsty for it!"

"You bet I am." So thirsty I could almost taste her swollen pussy lips against my tongue. "And you know what else I want to do?"

"What?" she asked.

I could see her naked breasts heaving as she rubbed her clit in her lonely hotel bed. I could picture the purse of her lips and that line across her forehead, the signs that she was so close, so close she could taste it.

"I want to get out a nice big dildo," I told her. "And I want to ram you so hard you can't take it anymore. I want you to feel that big cock all the way through you while I take your fat fucking clit between my lips and suck it until you scream my name."

"God, yes, Jackie." She screamed into the phone. "Yes, Jackie! YES!"

Her ecstasy summoned mine, and in seconds I was coming too, bucking my hips and clenching my ass cheeks. Holding my hips aloft, way up off the mattress, I scoured my clit in circles, then slapped it, scoured, then slapped. I started screaming into the phone, too, hollering, "Fuck yeah, Monique. Suck my clit, babygirl! You are so fucking hot!"

I could hear her gasping into the phone, and I knew she had her legs crossed tight together now, her hand still lodged between her thighs. She'd moved beyond bliss and taken me with her.

We lay together and apart, panting into our phones, saying nothing, struggling to catch our breath. We stayed that way for a good long time, and I felt myself drifting off until she asked, "Did you come?"

I laughed, of course, because I'd probably never come so hard in my life. "Yeah, babe, I came."

She said, "Good. I'm glad." And a moment later, "I came too."

"So I heard." There were so many things I loved about my woman, and the sound of her voice, her enthusiasm, those were high on the list. "I love talking dirty with you, Monique."

"I love talking with you, dirty or otherwise." She paused for a moment, then said, "But dirty *is* fun."

-20-
SPITE SEX

I still feel bad about this. I shouldn't have done it, no matter how angry I was. There's no excuse for cheating, but there are *reasons*. And here's mine.

Vicky and I were prone to the same kinds of arguments as straight couples, but when our hormones peaked, man oh man, we could tear a strip off one another. One Friday, we had a blow-out about nothing in particular. Vicky left my apartment, screaming, "Fuck you! Forget about your stupid concert!"

She was supposed to come to a little club downtown the next night, to watch a band I loved and she hated. When she said she wasn't coming, I believed her. Vicky was furious.

It just so happened that, two weeks before that argument, I'd received a pleading email from my ex-girlfriend. I broke up with Roma because she was way too intense for me, but she never gave up. She knew I was dating Vicky, but she didn't care. Roma didn't care about anyone but herself. I loved and hated her for that.

So, when Vicky and I had that huge fight, I thought, 'Fuck it! I'll invite Roma to the damn concert.' Maybe I needed to assert my independence, but more likely I just wanted to lash out. Vicky had said some really hurtful things, and I could never match her on name-calling.

But I could fuck someone else. There was no better revenge than spite sex.

The minute I spotted Roma outside that hole-in-the-wall tavern, my pussy pulsed—a thick throb, fast as my heartbeat. As I walked up to her, I could imagine the look on Vicky's face when I confessed to this. I couldn't wait to break her heart.

Roma grabbed me and I let her. We showed our tickets at the door, but my band wasn't up for another half-hour. As we crunched over peanut shells, Roma slid her lips across my cheek. I reminded her that I had a girlfriend. She said, "I don't care, and neither do you."

She was right. I asked her where, but that was a stupid question. She pulled me past the bar, and I followed like a dog on a short leash. My nipples were hard beneath my bra. I couldn't wait to feel her lips around them. Roma was such a great fuck, so passionate. I wanted her to take me.

Roma pulled me into the women's washroom, which was dingy as hell and only had two stalls. She kicked open the one that wasn't occupied, and slammed me inside, against the cold concrete wall. I could hardly breathe when she forced her lips against mine. I whimpered, but I didn't fight. After all, I wanted this.

The toilet in the next stall flushed, and I felt like such a slut, kissing my ex in a bathroom while some girl pissed next door. Roma grabbed at my corduroys, and when she couldn't get the fly undone fast enough, she ripped it open. I wasn't wearing any panties. Her hand found my heat quick as one-two-three. She attacked my pussy, shoving two fingers in my snatch and drawing my juice up, slathering it over my clit.

She was all over me, clutching my arm with one hand while the other smacked my clit. She spanked my cunt, slapped it. That thick pulse in my pussy had grown into something explosive.

Roma mashed her palm against me, and I screamed into her mouth. I couldn't even tell if there were other women in the bathroom, listening. When Roma rubbed my pussy hard and fast, I went wild, bucking like crazy, rubbing my wet cunt against her palm.

I don't know how she made me come so fast. I must have really wanted it, and the idea of hurting

Vicky was so horribly appealing that I just wanted more, more, more.

Pushing down on Roma's shoulders, I begged her to lick my snatch. I didn't need to ask twice. She dropped to her knees on that dirty bathroom floor and spread my pussy lips with her thumbs. It didn't matter that I'd just come. I could do it again. I could come a thousand times over, given the inspiration. And Roma was damn good at providing inspiration.

She didn't lick my clit. No. She shoved her fingers up my snatch, and then she sucked. This was my favourite of her moves—that come-hither motion she made against my G-spot while she sucked mercilessly at my fat little bud. I thrashed against the concrete wall and groaned as I rubbed my cunt against her face, spreading pussy juice all around her lips and down her chin.

When I told her I was going to come again, she only worked harder. She fucked me with her fingers and sucked me with her mouth. She went wild between my legs until I was hollering, cursing—I couldn't control myself.

I couldn't remember the last time I'd come so hard, and all I could see were my girlfriend's tears. I wanted her to cry when I told her about this. It would hurt her, right to the core.

I let Roma suck my clit until I couldn't stand the pleasure. Her hunger still wasn't satisfied, apparently. She rose to her feet and kissed me, fondling my breasts over my top until someone started pounding on the door, saying, "I have to pee, you stupid dykes!"

Roma strutted out of the stall. I slunk behind her, tying my hoodie around my waist to cover the rip in my pants.

When we left the bathroom, my band was just setting up. I couldn't wait to get some booze down my throat. Roma went to order at the bar, and the minute she stepped away, that's when I saw Vicky.

I could tell by the look on her face that she was sorry. I'd forgiven her a million times before, just like she'd forgiven me. When my eyes met hers I knew I couldn't fuck this relationship up. I ran to the door and wrapped my arms around her, pulling her outside, away from Roma.

Vicky was confused. She kept saying, "What about your band?" but staying for the concert was just asking for trouble. I'd used Roma to get back at Vicky, but all I could do was run away.

I never answered Roma's emails after that, and I never told Vicky what happened. Cheating out of spite is inexcusable. That's why I can't come clean.

All the same, every time I think about that dirty bathroom sex with Roma, I get a little thrill. It might have been wrong, but it felt damn good.

-21-
TASTE OF MY WOMAN

I pressed number one on my speed dial: *Monique Cell*. She picked up on the first ring. The phone bill was going to be astronomical this month.

"I only have a minute," I whispered, glancing around the office to make sure nobody was hovering too close. "Sid just got up to grab lunch, and he won't be gone for long. How's the conference going?"

Even over the phone, I could hear Monique shrug her shoulders. My woman was beautifully predictable with that sort of thing. "This city's full of politicians. I never know what to believe and what's spin."

Yes, I'd started it, but I realized right away I

didn't want to talk about work or spin or politics. "What are you doing right now?"

"Just ducking out of the lunch line to talk a little more… privately." Her voice deepened to satin gravel, shimmering and gorgeous and gritty all at once.

A moan slipped through my lips before I could catch it, and I looked around the office, but no one was about.

"Are you eating?" Monique asked. Not what I'd anticipated as an opening gambit, and I found the question jarring. "You don't eat enough, Jackie. I worry about you."

I sighed and said, "Well, *don't* worry—I'm eating," though it wasn't true. I hadn't called her for a lecture. Monique hadn't yet been away twenty-four hours, and already I was craving her presence, her body, her taste in my mouth.

"That's good," Monique replied. "I'm eating too. Here, I'll put a bite of this in your mouth and you tell me what it is."

Closing my eyes, I focused on the pleasured moan Monique released into my black Nortel phone receiver. Warm sweetness caressed my taste buds, and I knew precisely what she'd placed on my metaphysical tongue.

"You're eating dark chocolate. I can taste it." I peered down the hallway to make sure Sid wasn't on his way back. The coast was clear, and I was going all in. "Now, you tell me what I'm eating."

175

Monique gurgled, but answered without pause. "I know exactly what you're eating. You've got your face all up between my thighs, and you are just devouring my pussy."

"Yes I am, babygirl, and your pussy is delicious." There was a throb between my legs, like a drumbeat. We didn't do this. We didn't talk like this. Except now.

"Oh, you are sweet," Monique cooed. "Sweet as chocolate."

My eyelids fluttered closed. I wondered where she was, if she was alone now, if she was reaching inside her panties to play with her clit. God, I loved the image of my woman with her hand down her pants, slowly rubbing that sweet spot. I loved the image so much I was half tempted to slip my own fingers between my pussy lips and play in that liquid heat. But I couldn't do that…not at work…not sitting at my desk in my wide-open office…

"I'm kissing your mouth," I told Monique. Her little panting noises were getting the crotch of my panties incredibly slick with juice, but I wanted her words in my mouth. "Can you taste your pussy on my tongue?"

"Yes I can," she replied in a sizzling whisper. "It's mingling with the chocolate, like a dark chocolate pussy."

My breath hitched and I wanted so badly to slip a hand beneath my top, inside the cup of my bra, and pinch my nipples until they were hard as little pink pebbles. All I could do to resist was close my eyes and lick the picture Monique had planted in my mind. "Oh, your dark chocolate pussy is melting in my mouth...*and* in my hands." My head buzzed with sugar-coated arousal. "It's all over my fingers. The juice is running down my chin. Oh babygirl, your chocolate pussy is dripping all over me."

Monique gasped, and the sound sent a shock wave from my tits to my clit. "Tell me where," she begged. "Where's that chocolate dripping, Jackie?"

My name on her tongue was sweetest of all. "It's dripping all down my naked tits and you're sucking it from my nipples." I could feel my thighs squeezing together of their own volition, applying pressure to my fat clit peeking out from between two wet lips. I stifled a squeal.

"You lick it from my lips," she whispered. Her voice was a secret. "It's everywhere now. You suck the chocolate from my tongue and then sink right back down to suck it from my clit. My chocolate body is all over your skin, babydoll."

"My tongue is all over yours." I could see her now: the chocolate of her flesh melting with the heat of my lips on her engorged pussy lips, with the warmth of my hands on her smooth, dark thighs. She's all over my face. I'm messy with the taste of her.

"Lick me," she begged.

"Yes." My hand snuck up my thigh, pressing the seam of my neat grey slacks against my throbbing clit. The sensation was so startling my hips bucked forward before I could quell the motion. "God, babygirl, I'm getting off just imagining the taste of you."

"Me too."

And the idea that Monique was every bit as aroused as I was turned me on even more. It didn't take long. My imaginings had my clit thick and throbbing, just waiting for those little touches, one finger stroking my slacks. That's all I needed—I missed her so much. Her breath in the phone seemed sweet with chocolate, and my pleasure caught in my chest, a suppressed sound, thumping right there next to my heart, right there next to Monique. She was everything to me.

Sid cleared his throat and my pounding heart jumped out of my chest. When I pried my eyes open, he was standing in front of my desk with a grin plastered ear to ear. My skin prickled like it was breaking out in hives. Embarrassment didn't even begin to describe what I was feeling in that moment. My face must have been glowing crimson.

"I have to go, Monique." I didn't want to tell her why.

"Tastus Interuptus?" Her lustful giggle spoke volumes, and I stared down at the keypad on the phone to keep Sid out of my field of vision. I wanted just this, just five more seconds alone with my woman before we had to hang up.

"I love you," I said. It came out as a whimper.

"You too, kid." The smile in Monique's voice made me flush all over again. "Now get yourself some food. You need more for lunch than a single helping of long-distance pussy."

-22-
TERRITORY

I walked ahead while she danced behind me, both hands lodged between her thighs.

"I gotta pee," she whimpered, like it pained her to speak. "I'm serious, Kate. This isn't funny."

"It's funny to me," I shot back, turning around to enjoy her torment. "My mom used to call that *the potty dance.*"

Aliyah bit her lip. "Shut up! Don't make me laugh."

The way her face contorted as she struggled not to leak made me love her all the more, if that was even possible. Everything Aliyah did or said turned me on to some degree, and I knew she knew, but she wouldn't take the bait. It didn't seem to matter how funny I was or how charming, or how much money I spent treating her to take-out and bad movies—my roommate didn't like me the way I liked her. And it frustrated the hell out of me.

"Okay," I teased, backing her up against the brickwork. The bus route on our stupid street didn't run after nine at night, so we were walking—almost home, but not close enough. "I'll just tickle you instead. How 'bout that?"

A sheet of rage flashed across Aliyah's face. "Touch me and I'll kill you, Kate."

"*I'll Kill You, Kate*: Cole Porter's lesser-known classic."

"Shut up, oh my God!" Aliyah covered her mouth and crossed her legs, leaning back against the side of our corner store, struggling to contain herself. "I'm gonna piss my pants."

If the most ardent emotion I could provoke from her was anger, so be it.

"Go ahead." I poked her and she hit my hand away, so I came at her from the other side, making her shriek. "I dare you to pee right here. Just do it."

The fury in her eyes melted into pain. That's when I knew I had her.

She cupped her hands around her crotch, whispering, "Nooo…"

I could pants her pretty easily, and I knew she'd be furious. If only she'd worn short shorts like me I could just pull the crotch to one side of her pussy, but Aliyah always wore long sleeves and pants for the same reason she wore a hijab. So I grabbed the waistband of her pants, slid my fingers between her soft skin and her panties, and pulled them both down so hard she screamed.

Everything seemed to happen at once after that. I stood up instinctively, even though I wanted to get a closer look at her crotch. Her black hair was neat and trim, and her pinkish pussy lips jutted out from within that manicured slit. God, I wanted to dive between her thighs and gnaw at her clit, but this obviously wasn't the time. She was going to burst any second now.

"What the fuck?" Aliyah shouted, shielding her pussy from my hungry eyes.

I grabbed her wrists and jerked them back against the brick wall. She let me do it. Aliyah was way stronger than me, so when she gave in without a struggle, I knew what she wanted.

"Piss on me." I moved closer, so my bare legs almost touched hers. "Do it. Piss on my thigh."

"Fuck, Kate!" Her voice was a growl. She sounded like an animal, and still she didn't struggle. "Stop it."

Only one thing left to do: I pressed my naked thigh between her legs, spreading her wet pussy lips and rubbing until she whimpered.

"You gotta piss, right?" Oh, I felt like such a bitch doing this to her. "So piss. Go ahead. Just do it."

Turning her head away from me, she muttered, "I can't…"

But she could, and she did, releasing a forceful stream of piss against my thigh.

The warmth struck me first, followed by the scent, which was familiar and yet so wonderfully Aliyah that it turned me on as much as anything else about her.

I watched her stream hit my thigh and drizzle down my leg, dripping off my bent knee and onto the sidewalk. The drip-drip-drip as her pee hit the concrete made me weak, and when I gazed into her eyes, the look I found there was dark and unfamiliar.

When I let go of Aliyah's wrists, her stream died down against my leg. She reached for my arms, grabbing them right up near my shoulders, squeezing. Her piss was already drying against my skin, cooling on the night air, but I couldn't look away from her huge eyes with those lashes like dark blades. I fixated on her. She was everything to me, and she was so, so close.

"I can't believe I just did that," she whispered. "I can't believe I pissed on you."

The night seemed extra quiet now, and for the first time I wondered what might happen if someone caught us.

"That's fine," I said, teasing even though I was dead serious. "You were just marking your territory."

Without another word, Aliyah pulled me so close my breasts mashed against hers. Before I could process how much that sensation turned me on, her lips were on mine, her tongue prying open my shocked mouth. She kissed me intently, unrelentingly, squeezing my arms like I'd run away if she didn't hold on tight.

Pressing her against the brick wall, I returned her kiss tenfold, pushing my thigh against her wet pussy. When she started not just rubbing but grinding her clit against me, I shivered with lust.

Her pussy lips played against my smooth skin, gliding up and down my thigh. "Yeah," I said. "Come for me, 'liyah. Rub that hot little cunt all over me, baby."

Aliyah whimpered as she stroked off on me. I could only imagine how hard her clit was throbbing as she scoured my thigh. Her motions got jerky as her breath came on stronger. She was thrusting now, rude and crude, throwing herself against me like a dog humping its owner's leg. Shameless. I didn't know she had it in her.

I'd heard Aliyah come before, but never so close, and never for me. This time when she whispered, "Yes, yes, yes!" right against my lips, I knew this was only the beginning.

She pulled away from our kiss, her hips still thrusting, fucking my thigh. "Yes!" She howled so loud I had to cover her yap.

That didn't stop her from shouting, though. She panted a continuous string of, "Yes, yes, yes!" against my palm. Each one sounded thready and tortured, like the effort to speak was just too much.

She closed her eyes. The muscles in her neck strained as she arched up the wall. "Oh, fuck!"

Aliyah pushed me away, covering her poor mound, gasping desperately. She looked me in the eye, a wounded animal. Her gaze grew stern but her voice was breathless, even gauzy, when she finally asked, "Can I be your territory, Kate?"

After all this time, all my relentless pursuits, this was all it took? One golden shower and an orgasm?

"Territory!" I could have laughed, but instead I cupped my hand over hers. I squeezed her mound as we kissed. "That's all I ever wanted."

-23-
THE THINGS SHE SAYS

The things my girl says when she's out West and I'm back East, boy, they melt me like butter!

And usually her saucy ideas come out of nowhere. We're just talking about whatever, chatting on the phone, and suddenly—bang!—my panties are slick and I'm counting the minutes until she gets home.

Like the other day... well, I guess I started it the other day. We were talking about what she had for dinner, what I had for dinner, then about cooking and all that. I remember she said, "Cooking is skill and art. Baking is skill and chemistry."

I said, "I like to improvise. That's why I'm better at cooking than baking. When I bake I have to be disciplined."

It wasn't until after I'd said it that I heard the double meaning. I was really just talking about using measuring spoons instead of eyeballing it.

But I think Becca took a shine to that word, *discipline*, because she laughed her throaty laugh—the one that tells me she's got ideas in her head—and she asked, "Why do you think I bought you a brand new wooden spoon?"

I knew what she meant, but I wanted to hear her say it. "Why, Becca?"

She laughed some more and said, "So you can be *disciplined* while you bake!"

That's exactly what I thought she was going to say, but I still blushed. Even though my girl was all the way across the country and could only see my pretty face in her mind's eye, my cheeks burned red. And I giggled.

"Or would you rather have me tie you up?" she asked. "How about that, sugar? Tie you up and whack you with that spoon!"

I was lying on my couch, and still my legs were trembling up a storm. My skin was twitching for her, wanting her here to warm my ass.

"That sounds good," I said. "Wish you could smack me right now."

I heard her breath change the way it always does when I moan about something I can't have. But she recovered without scolding me, without telling me she does the best she can or that her work's important too. She stayed in the game and said, "Maybe one day I'll bind you up really tight so you can hardly move, then I'll eat you 'til you can't breathe enough to say stop."

"Yes," I begged. "Please do that."

"I'll bend your knees and tie your ankles around your thighs…"

"Yes, please." My toes were curling already.

"…and I'll tie your hands at your sides. No, I'll attach them to your ankles. How about that?"

"Oh my god!" Between my legs, I was wet and ready. She was talking about tying me up, but that didn't mean I had to deny myself the pleasure right now. Did it?

"How about a short dowel under each knee as I tie you? That would keep your knees apart."

I said, "Okay," even though I couldn't really picture what she meant. Part of what turned me on so much was just the sound of her voice: husky and dark. It got inside me like a tornado, whirling around in my belly.

"Good position to eat you," she said. "Eat you, finger you, fist you, fuck you…"

"You're making me so horny!" There was no other word for it. My pussy pounded. I think it was the mention of fisting that really put me over the edge—and then wondering what she'd use to fuck me.

"Sorry for making you horny," she teased.

"Vixen!" I teased back. "I'm clawing my eyes out,

here."

"A couple light plastic bulldog clips with not much pressure, but enough to attach to each nipple."

My tits knew they'd been mentioned. They started throbbing just as hard as my pussy. "Oh God," I said. "That would hurt."

Her voice was low like black velvet. "No, baby, just light clips."

"They would still hurt," I said. "But that's the point, right? The pain is pleasure."

I listened to her breath—a heavy, heaving rattle. What was she doing all the way out there? Did she spend as much time thinking of me as I spent thinking of her? That question was always on my mind, but I never asked. I didn't want her to know how needy I was in my heart of hearts.

So instead of talking about relationship matters, I said, "I love it when you do stuff to my nipples."

"Oh, do you?" she asked with a shimmering giggle. "Well, baby, after you're all tied up I'll show you the biggest fucking cucumber in the world."

I felt my eyes widen as my pussy pulsed. "Oh my god. I hope you do more than just show me."

Her chuckle felt a little more cruel this time. "A cucumber and a whole bottle of really good lube."

"Oh!" My clit felt so huge and distended it actually started to ache inside my panties. "You must be as horny as I am, or else you're just trying to torture me."

"Wait until I bring home that cucumber," she

said. "That's when I'll really torture you."

"Yes, please."

"And that new wooden spoon? I could fuck you with one end and spank your ass and your nipples with the other."

"And spank my pussy too?" I cupped my mound with one hand and squeezed. It felt so good I groaned into the phone, wondering what her hands were up to.

"And your pussy," she agreed. "If that's what you like—if you want to get your pussy all red and spanked. If you want to get your pussy juice all over your brand new wooden spoon."

"Oh!" I slid my palm down, nestling it firmly against my clit, and started rocking on my hand. "I'm squirming, baby. You're making me wild."

"You would be wild if I were smacking your slit with a wooden spoon."

She never used to be like this, my Becca. When we first met, she was my little vanilla cupcake. Now she was full of ideas, and anxious to turn those ideas into action.

"Did I make you this way?" I asked. "Did I turn you into a kinkster?"

"A little," she said. "But it's more like you made it possible for me imagine things and then tell you about them. You're my safe space. You're not going to judge me."

"No, I won't." I closed my eyes and grinded against my hand, imagining I was getting off on her tongue. "Even when you're all the way across the country and I want you between my legs, I still won't judge you, Becca."

She was quiet for a moment, and I knew she was trying to decode my tone. Passive-aggressive? Is that how she heard it? Is that how I meant it? Sometimes even I didn't know.

"I want you home," I said to fill the void.

"Ahhh." Becca's smile was right there in her voice. I could see her face between my thighs. I could see her smiling up at me. "Thanks. That's a nice compliment."

I writhed against my palm, but I wasn't going to come tonight, not without my girl. "I wish you were here so I could fuck you right now and then wake you up in the morning."

"Wake me up how?" she asked.

"With my mouth, of course."

"Nice." Her voice was softer, a dove's otherworldly coo.

I said, "You're my girl. I know what you like."

"Yes you do." She breathed heavily, and then said, "Go to sleep, sugar. It's late where you are."

Three hours' time difference between Becca and me. I couldn't help wondering how she'd fill the void.

"Wish you were here," I said.

She replied, "I know," which wasn't the same as saying, "I wish that too."

We were quiet while I tried working up the

courage to ask if she had another girl out West. But I'd always been a weakling. I couldn't ask a question like that. I didn't want to know.

"Dream of me," she said.

"Oh, trust me, Becca." I pulled my wet hand out of my panties and wiped it on the dirty couch. "Trust me, I will."

-24-

UNDERHANDED

I once asked my girlfriend, "Do you ever wonder what a lesbian glory hole would look like?"

She laughed, of course. Kendra always laughs when I say stuff like that.

"It couldn't be a hole in a wall," she said, "because what would lesbians stick through it?"

"You could stick your tongue through a hole in the wall," I replied with a shrug.

She disagreed. "That wouldn't work. No way you could give oral through a hole."

Okay, so she was probably right about that. Even if it was possible, it would definitely be awkward.

"Well," I said, "one could bend over and press her pussy to the hole, and then the girl on the other side could fingerfuck her."

But Kendra shook her head. "Women wouldn't do that, not with strangers."

I wasn't so sure, but it's easier not to argue.

The next time we found ourselves together in a public washroom, it just happened to be at our favourite restaurant. After settling the bill, Kendra ducked into the bathroom to pee and I followed along. Though there were five stalls in total, I couldn't recall ever seeing any other patrons using them.

Kendra took the first stall and I walked down to the other end to give her space. When I got to the end of the row, she called my name in that seductive sing-song voice of hers. My heart beat fast as I turned to see what she wanted. I think I already knew.

"Don't go so far," she said. "Come, get in the stall next to me."

No way could I resist, not with the way she was grinning at me. So I retraced my steps, slipping into the stall beside Kendra's. After padding the toilet seat with paper, I pulled up my skirt, dropped my panties and peed while my girl did the same.

Just as I was wiping myself, a hand appeared underneath the divider wall between my stall and Kendra's. I took one look at those fingers and their "come hither" motion, and I burst out laughing.

"You're not serious," I said.

"Why not?" Her hand stayed put, but her fingers

kept moving, beckoning my pussy.

I looked at the structure of the stall itself, but the stainless steel walls between stalls were higher up from the floor than the doors were. "What if someone walks in?"

"Then you just stand up when you hear the door open," my girlfriend said. "They'd never know."

This was a nice restaurant, and the bathroom seemed very clean: nice slate floors, no toilet paper on the ground. Kendra was right—nobody would ever know—so how could I object?

With my panties around my ankles and my skirt bunched up over my hips, I leaned my back against the cold wall and inched my way down into a squat. My thighs trembled even before my pussy landed smack in Kendra's outreached hand. When I felt her fingers brushing my pubic hair, my whole body quaked. I hissed, "Oh my God!" even though I was trying to be quiet.

She said, "Shh!" no doubt to tease me while her fingers found my slit. It never took me long to get wet, and there was something about squatting inches from the floor in a public bathroom that really got my juices flowing. By the time she started smacking my cunt, giving me sharp little spankings against my naked pussy lips, I was dripping all over her hand.

My tender flesh sizzled from the slaps, and I yelped with every one. My thighs shook so hard they barely kept me up, but I pressed my back against the wall and my hands against my knees, and hoped I wouldn't fall and smack my pussy on the floor.

I don't know why I was surprised when Kendra stopped spanking me. The sharp sensation was becoming unbearable, but I inexplicably wanted more. And then she pressed a finger into my wet snatch, and I couldn't have cared less about spankings. I wanted this now. I wanted my girl to fingerfuck me… hard!

"Fuck, you are so tight!" Kendra said through the wall.

There was something about that word, tight, that made me clench even harder around her finger. It's not something she said very often. In fact, I couldn't remember her ever telling me I was tight before.

"Say that again," I begged as she somehow managed to get another finger inside my unyielding slit.

"Tight," she whispered. She moved in me so slowly I could hardly stand the suspense. "God, girl, you are damn tight."

My thighs were killing me, and I winced at the pain in my muscles, but I didn't want Kendra to stop. Two fingers had never felt so huge, and I knew it was all about this strange position, perched so close to the floor I could feel the chilly air coming off the cool stone tiles.

As Kendra moved her fingers faster inside my wet pussy, I wanted to fuck them back, to drop down on that unrelenting girth, but I knew if I tried to move even an inch, I was sure to collapse.

"That feel good?" she asked, like it was a real question, like she wasn't sure if I was into this and she really needed to know.

The sound that came from my throat was a whimper of a yes, barely there though I wanted to scream it at the top of my lungs. The wet squelch of my cunt spoke for me as her fingers fucked my pussy even harder than before. They wanted me to come. Kendra had me at that brink, and she wanted to toss me over.

I wanted it, too.

My pussy hugged those fingers hard, and I wondered what Kendra was doing over there with one spare hand. Was she playing with her clit, or focusing all her energy on me? My thighs trembled like crazy, shaking so hard I had to reach up and grab hold of the toilet paper dispenser. That gave me just enough leverage to grind down on Kendra's hand, milking my favourite fingers as they fucked me.

I was getting there fast, and I knew exactly what would push me over that cliff. With my skirt still bunched up over my waist, I let my fingers slip down between my legs. My clit pulsed when I touched it, sending streaks of electricity through my pussy. I was hanging off the toilet paper holder now, so low to the ground the back of Kendra's hand smacked the floor, but she kept on fucking me.

"Yes!" I hissed over and over again. Scouring my clit, I banged Kendra's fingers, squeezing them hard with my tense pussy muscles. "Yes, yes, yesssss…"

It was then the door squeaked open and a pair of heels click-clacked across the floor.

I froze.

My mind was saying, "Get up, stupid! Stand up now!" but my whole body went into spasm. It wasn't until Kendra slipped her fingers from my pussy that I managed to pull myself up. The footsteps outside didn't slow and that woman didn't say anything, so I'm sure she didn't know what we were up to. Even so, my heart was racing and I had to lean against the wall to stay on me feet.

"Well?" Kendra said, winking at me in the mirror as we washed our hands side by side.

"Well?" I teased, winking back at her.

"What did you think of that?"

"That…" I shook the water from my fingertips and then grabbed a paper towel. "…was underhanded."

The End

ABOUT THE AUTHOR

Giselle Renarde is a queer Canadian, contributor to more than 100 short story anthologies, and award-winning author of dozens of electronic and print books, including *Anonymous, Cherry, Seven Kisses, Nanny State, What Do Lesbians Do In Bed?* and the *Wedding Heat* series. Giselle lives across from a park with two bilingual cats who sleep on her head.

Ms. Renarde's anthology *My Mistress' Thighs: Erotic Transgender Fiction and Poetry* received an Honourable Mention in the 2011 Rainbow Awards, and her trans lesbian romance *The Red Satin Collection* took top prize in the same category in 2012. She is a contributor to Tristan Taormino's Lambda Award-winning book *Take Me There: Trans and Genderqueer Erotica*, as well as such notable anthologies as Best Women's Erotica, Best Lesbian Erotica, Best Bondage Erotica, and Best Lesbian Romance.

Find Giselle online at
http://donutsdesires.blogspot.com or on Twitter
@GiselleRenarde.

For discounts, freebie alerts and updates, sign up to receive Giselle's newsletter: http://eepurl.com/R4b11

Printed in Great Britain
by Amazon